ALICE'S ALPHAS

SHIFTER MENAGE ROMANCE

ANN GIMPEL

Edited by
ANGELA KELLY
Illustrated by
FIONA JAYDE

CONTENTS

ALICE'S ALPHAS

WOLF CLAN SHIFTERS, BOOK ONE

Shifter Ménage Romance
By
Ann Gimpel

One virgin + three wolf shifters = e-reader ecstasy

Copyright Page

All rights reserved.
Copyright © July 2013, Ann Gimpel
Cover Art Copyright © February 2016, Fiona Jayde
Edited by: Angela Kelly
Names, characters, and incidents depicted in this book are products of the author's imagination, or are used fictitiously. Any resemblance to actual events, locales, organizations, or people living or dead, is entirely coincidental and beyond the intent of the author.
No part of this book may be reproduced or shared by any

electronic or mechanical means, including but not limited to printing, file sharing, e-mail, or web posting without written permission from the author.

Publishing history: This book was released by Liquid Silver Books as *Alice's Alpha* in July 2013. A substantively rewritten version, *Alice's Alphas*, was released by Ann Gimpel and Dream Shadow Press in March 2016.
ISBN: 978-1-948871-17-4

It's 1936. Thirty-year-old Alice has given up on finding a husband. Between civil engineering and mountain climbing, her interests are so masculine, she scares men away. A poor route choice strands her—lost, hungry, and scared—next to Lon Chaney's cabin deep in the Sierra Nevada Mountains.

Jed senses a woman stumbling down the steep, inhospitable mountain behind his borrowed cabin. Her scent tantalizes and excites him. Mates are scarce these days, and if his nose is right, she's his fated one. His and his two pack mates, that is, who are mercifully gone at the moment. Jed crafts a careful strategy, knowing the mate bond might not be enough to convince her to stay once she finds out it will link her to all three of them—forever.

Alice adds Jed to her list of problems when he melts out of the shadowed darkness. At first she declines his offer of help, but he keeps talking until she ends up inside the cozy log cabin in front of a roaring fire. His skilled hands and a shot of whiskey heat her blood to molten, and her carefully tended world explodes into desperate hunger to make love with the man rubbing her weary feet.

As caught up in lust as Alice, Jed takes a chance. A big one. Will mating with her before disclosing everything turn out to be a huge mistake?

CHAPTER 1

"This way, Alice." Brent chugged downhill. His tall, well-muscled frame dislodged small boulders and mini snow avalanches. Longish red hair was escaping from the piece of cloth he'd tied around it.

"I don't think that's right," she protested and dug her crampon points into the steep slope more firmly. The metal spikes didn't stay very well because the snow was too soft. She looked at the angle of the sun, nearly hidden by the steep flanks of an unnamed peak. Hardly any of the Sierra peaks had names. The one they'd just climbed certainly didn't.

Damn!

It would be dark in less than an hour. Even though it was early March, days were still short.

"I tell you, this route will work," floated up to her.

"Bullshit! It's suicide," she shouted back.

"You have the skill for this. Just take your time. There's something I, um, need to do, I'll wait for you on the far side of the creek. If you don't find me, head for the car as fast as you can. Lock yourself in if you're too tired to drive."

"What?" Her throat tightened. "You can't just leave me. It'll be dark soon."

"You'll be fine, Alice. We're past the worst of things, and I don't have any choice." The sound of him thrashing downhill nearly obliterated his last words.

She clamped her teeth together. What the hell had he meant about heading for the car as fast as she could? Maybe he was losing it. She'd read about climbers who edged into madness, but today hadn't been that difficult.

She was cold and tired too, and convinced they were lost. Their ascent route hadn't been all that great, so Brent suggested they try a more direct line going down. The first thousand feet had worked fine, then they'd run into a band of cliffs. She glanced up. It did seem the cliffs were above them now, but the terrain was perilously steep. She jammed her ice axe into the slope and turned face in. Brent may have been comfortable barreling down like one of the rocks he'd displaced, but she wasn't.

Alice moved carefully. She planted her axe into the slope, and then found lower purchase for both feet. It took a while. By the time she moved off the steepest part, it was nearly full dark. She cupped her hands around her mouth and called, "Brent."

He didn't answer. She yelled his name again. Silence. Panic made her heart thud dully against her ribs, its echo loud in her ears. She felt sick and dizzy. They should've taken the known route down. Why had she let him talk her into something so foolish, especially with so little of the day left?

And what was so all-fired important he had to go off and leave her?

Alice slid her rucksack off her shoulders and felt around for her calcium carbide lantern. She poured a little of her precious water into the lantern's upper compartment, gave it a moment, and flashed the flint. The lantern flickered and sputtered, but then a warm, blue flame steadied. She drank some water and worked at convincing herself not to think too much while she clipped the light to a broad band and settled it around her head. Shouldering her pack, she picked her way downhill.

After about an hour, thick timber surrounded her. The terrain had eased off to maybe thirty degrees. Fallen branches crisscrossed over one another were more of a problem now than steepness. She dropped below the snowline and sat on a downed log to take off her crampons. They snagged on things, reducing her already-slow progress. Bundling the steel spikes, she secured them to her pack, and then called Brent's name again.

And again.

Anger gave way to fear something hideous had happened. He'd careened down the slope like a madman, but she hadn't heard him scream. Surely, she'd have heard something if he'd fallen. His exhortation about heading for the car rattled in the back of her mind.

Was there some sort of danger she wasn't aware of? Was that why he'd abandoned her? She shook her head. It didn't make sense. If danger lurked nearby, he should've stayed to protect her, not taken off like a bat out of hell.

Alice shivered. The temperature was somewhere south of freezing. Her wool top, jacket, and pants were wet with sweat on the inside and wet from falling in the snow so many times on the outside. Between the two, it would take hours for the thick cloth to dry. Thank God it wasn't windy. Wind-chill would add to her woes. She set her lantern off to one side so its hiss wouldn't drown out something important and listened.

The welcome sound of water cascading over stones sounded from below. If she just kept on downhill, she had to come to the North Fork of Big Pine Creek. "Even if it's the

South Fork, it's not the end of the world," she muttered. "Come daylight, I'll recognize something."

She settled her lantern back in place and pulled a pair of wool mitts out of her pack. When she got to her feet, she groaned. Everything hurt, but tomorrow would be worse once her over-taxed muscles stiffened up. Cursing under her breath, she gathered her things together and worked her way through increasingly thick deadfall. As she down climbed, she thought about Brent. All they were, really, was friends. She'd tried to make it more than that, to flirt with him, but he'd never been interested. He made a most excellent climbing partner, though.

At least he had until today.

None of the women she knew had the least interest in the mountains, and men thought it unwomanly for her to don climbing regalia and take to the hills—except Brent. He understood the pull of the Sierras and didn't think it at all odd she felt the same. She pressed her tongue against her teeth. It was the nineteen-thirties, after all. Women were more than baby machines and unpaid cooks and housekeepers. She'd been practically the only female in many of her college classes, especially the math and science ones. Even with a degree, it hadn't been easy to get a job in civil engineering.

"It's not your credentials," she'd been told over and over. "You're just going to get married and all the time and money we put into training you will go to waste."

She'd been so grateful to the Orange County firm that finally hired her, she'd come perilously close to breaking into tears. Alice shook her head, but gently. No point in making the lantern go out. It was heavy strapped to her head. She'd be glad to get to somewhere she could stop for the night. She called Brent's name every few minutes. If he'd been knocked unconscious, maybe something would get through since hearing was the last sense to go.

The sound of rushing water grew louder, so loud she worried how she'd get across it. If it was the right creek, and it pretty much had to be, the trail was on the other side. She and Brent had crossed the turbulent flow using a rough wooden bridge much farther up the narrow canyon. The hillside steepened again. If it got any worse, she'd need to face into the hill to keep going.

She stopped on the uphill side of a fat tree bole long enough to lash her axe to her pack to free both hands. Alice used thick timber to control her descent, wrapping her hands around branches to keep herself from sliding down the muddy mountainside. Bark poked through her mitts and hurt her hands.

"Holy shit."

She tightened her fingers reflexively on slick bark. The creek, running at close to flood stage from an early snowmelt, was right below her. She'd nearly fallen into it. Her heart raced. She'd been careful, but she was tired. Too tired to be in a place where every step required thought. Water swirled around huge boulders ten feet below her. No way in hell to cross there. She looked downstream, but she couldn't see very far. The beam from her lamp was broad rather than deep. It looked like the water disappeared into a cascade, though.

Only one choice left.

Alice picked her way upstream over bushes and branches, staying as close to the creek as she could. Her strength was nearly at its end, and she felt ill and shaky. She hadn't let herself dwell on animals that might attack or Brent being dead, but both rose to taunt her. Just when she was considering getting out her rope and lashing herself to a tree to sit out the night, the angle of the slope eased and she found herself in a small meadow.

The water was still rushing fast, but the terrain was level

enough, she could cross here if she was careful. Several flat stones looked promising, though they might be slippery. Alice looked around for something to sit on. She needed to take off her pack to unstrap her axe. She'd need it for balance crossing the creek.

"I should eat and drink something," she murmured, understanding how close to the end of her tether she was. She called Brent's name again, but the noise of the water obliterated her voice.

She shucked her pack, got a glass water bottle, and bent near the water's edge to fill it. Alice drained the bottle and filled it once more, then staggered back to her meager stack of supplies. She blew out her lantern to conserve fuel. She didn't have any more of the calcium carbide crystals, and she'd need light to cross the water. She gathered her thick, heavy dark hair and braided it to get it out of the way. Lacking something to secure it with, she stuffed the end of the braid under her jacket. The thought of the trail—and safety—less than two hundred yards from her was seductive, but she knew better than to rush things. Climbers who got in a hurry ended up dead.

Brent, oh Brent...

His tall, broad-shouldered frame and sparkling green eyes rose before her. Even if he hadn't wanted to date her, they'd been the best of friends and she'd miss him terribly—if the unspeakable had happened.

Yeah, if he's dead, I suppose I'll have to forgive him for running off and leaving me. But if he's not, I'm going to give that man a piece of my mind.

Her gaze scanned the darkness. She blinked and looked again. A light shone through the trees across the creek. Joy swooped through her.

Brent.

He was okay after all and had set up camp to wait for her. Drawn by the prospect of not being alone anymore, she bundled the rest of her food and stuffed it into her rucksack. When she settled the pack over her shoulders, it rubbed on sore spots, but she ignored the pain shooting down her back and upper arms.

Soon. I can take it off for a few hours very soon.

The lantern was fussy. She had to clean some of the sludge out of the lower chamber to get it to light. Finally, with the lantern on her forehead and the axe in one hand, she set out for the far side of the creek. If she got really lucky, her feet wouldn't get any wetter than they already were in their clunky, two-layer, leather climbing boots. She blessed her six-foot frame. If she'd been smaller—more woman-sized—she'd never have found climbing clothes to fit. Bespoke tailoring was expensive.

Alice kept her gaze on the light. By the time she was halfway across the water, she knew it wasn't a fire. The beam was too steady. No, it burned like an electric light, or a kerosene lantern. That gave her pause. Her earlier elation faded. Probably not Brent. Maybe some hunters who'd packed a camp in with mules or horses.

If it's a bunch of men, they can help hunt for Brent come morning.

She moved from rock to rock, sinking her long-handled axe into the riverbed for support. It was easier than she'd thought. The last rock wobbled, but she caught herself and leapt to the far bank. The water was a few inches deep, but didn't slop over her boot tops. Alice didn't take time to congratulate herself on making it to safety. She headed for the light. A thick stand of trees blocked her vision momentarily, but she kept moving in a straight line. Fifty feet past the trees, she saw a cabin set in a glade. The light was indeed a kerosene lantern hanging from a hook near the door.

Her eyes widened. Lon Chaney's cabin. She and Brent had passed it on their way in. The thick fieldstone walls were unmistakable. The story of how Lon Chaney, Senior, had built it around 1930, using mules to drag the huge fieldstones the last distance after the road ended, was legendary. A shudder ran down her back, followed by another. All the creepy roles played first by Lon Chaney, and then by his son, poured through her mind.

I'm just tired. It's only a cabin.

Yes, but who lit the lantern?

Suddenly cautious, Alice turned the dial to douse her light. It made a small whumping sound and went out. She faded into the stand of trees between the cabin and the river and worked her way around to the other side of the building looking for evidence of hunters. A complete transit of the cabin with no horses or mules tethered for the night scared the shit out of her. Had whoever was inside come on foot? How had they carried enough supplies?

Her breath whistled loud in her ears. Brent had told her to hightail it for the car, but she had a feeling something bad had happened to him. No matter how she felt about him running off, it wasn't right to just leave him. It had been dark for hours, and she wondered how late it was. Even if she stumbled the few miles to her car waiting next to Glacier Lodge, she was too tired to drive anywhere. The lodge wasn't any help. It wouldn't open for the season for another couple of months. There might be a phone inside, but she'd have to break in.

Alice considered her options. If she made the lodge, she'd crawl into her car and fall on her face from exhaustion. It would easily be mid-morning before she got back up here to even begin searching for Brent. Survival in the mountains often hung by a thread. She was the only one who knew where he was.

He may have abandoned her, but she couldn't do the same and desert him. Not and live with herself afterward.

Alice moved toward where she thought the trail was, intent on setting up a fireless camp to wait out the night. She had enough food and a full water bottle. No tent or sleeping bag, but she'd survived worse conditions. A fire would've been welcome, but she couldn't risk—

"Hey there. You. Show yourself, man," a deep voice called from behind her. Light flared, illuminating the forest. Foot-steps crunched over rocks and twigs as the person approached.

Alice stiffened. People looked at her build and assumed she was male. It had happened to her before—and more than once. She considered running, but burdened with her heavy boots, climbing hardware, and the moonless night, she didn't want to chance a headlong flight. Besides, the man might have a gun.

"Why should I?" She spun to face him, ready for almost anything.

"What? You're a woman?"

Alice grasped her ice axe in both hands. "Leave me alone," she grunted through clenched teeth. "I'm tired and my friend is...lost."

"Whoa." The man held up both hands, one of which gripped a flashlight. "Put your axe down, sweetheart. I'm not going to hurt you." He was tall, maybe six-feet-four, with straight, red-blonde hair. Despite his height, he had a slender build. A well-defined jaw and sharp cheekbones suggested Nordic blood. It was tough to tell in the reflected light, but his eyes looked blue.

"Go back inside. You can see I'm not any kind of threat. I'd head down, but I need to be moving at first light to hunt for my friend."

The man cocked his head to one side. "Big guy with red hair?"

Terror gripped her. Her throat narrowed. Breathing became a struggle. Since she couldn't manage words, she nodded and steeled herself to hear the words, *he's dead.* Alice bit her lower lip and gazed mutely at the stranger.

"Look, I think he'll be okay. We were out hunting and heard something big falling. Thought it was the deer we'd shot at. Turned out to be your friend—"

"Awk! You shot Brent!"

The man waved his hands in front of him. "Calm down, woman. Christ, you're strung tighter than a fiddle. Take a couple of deep breaths. No, we didn't shoot him. Your friend was unconscious because he hit his head on a rock, so we carried him back here. My two buddies took the horses and hauled him down to the lodge. We only had three horses which is why I'm still here. Anyway, they were planning to drive him to the hospital in Bishop. I don't expect they'll be back much before the middle of tomorrow."

At least that explains why there're no horses here.

Alice shook her head, digesting the information. "I need to get moving, then. I can drive to the hospital and meet them."

The man held out a hand. "I'm Jed. Jed Starnes. You look beat. There're mountain cats on the prowl. Shot one a few hours ago. They get worse at night. More aggressive. You got a gun?"

She shook her head and ignored his outstretched hand. He looked chagrined and dropped it to his side. "Well, then, handshake or no, you need to come with me. Got a nice warm fire going inside. You look wet clear through. Nothing you can do tonight, anyway. Get a few shots of Irish whiskey in you, a little soup, and some sleep. Come morning, you can go after your friend."

It sounded good. Too good. She kept her ice axe poised. "How'd you get access to Lon Chaney's cabin?"

Jed threw back his head and laughed. "That's easy. Ever since Chaney senior died in nineteen-thirty, his son's been letting some of us who work with him have the keys. All we have to do is ask. Damn shame the old man died right after he got this place built. It's a beauty. You really should take a look inside."

She blew out a breath. "What is it you do?"

"I'm a production manager for Paramount."

"I thought they were in receivership."

He laughed again. "We are. But we're still making movies."

Something about Jed put her at ease. Or maybe she was just too weary to think straight. She slowly dropped her hands. Tethered to her wrist, the ice axe dangled, not quite hitting the ground.

"That's better, sweetheart," he crooned. "Follow me. I promise I don't bite."

She trailed after him and climbed the broad steps leading to the cabin's heavy wooden door. He unlatched it, took the lantern from its hook, and motioned her through ahead of him. Alice scanned the large room. One end was an enormous stone fireplace. The other held a kitchen of sorts with a pump mounted next to a sink. A curtained alcove probably contained a bedroom. The lower walls were the same large, flat fieldstones mortared together she'd seen on the outside. The upper walls were wooden planks. Alice sighed. It was warm. Truly warm. She didn't realize how chilled she was. Her face stung from the sudden temperature shift.

She took off her headlamp and set it on a table. Next she unbuckled her waist belt and dropped her pack in a corner, followed by her axe. The click of a deadbolt falling into its metal hole snapped her to attention. She made a grab for her axe, but Jed beat her to it. "Don't know about you," he said, hefting the axe over a shoulder, "but I'm not fond of weapons inside."

She'd been right about his eyes. They were a rich midnight blue. Something about them made her tingle deep inside. Alice pushed the thought away. She was still a virgin at nearly thirty, and likely to stay that way at the rate things were going in her life. Almost as if they'd been listening in on her thoughts, her nipples pebbled into points of awareness.

What am I doing?

She shook herself back to reality. A stranger she'd just met had locked her into this cabin and taken her only means of defense. Trepidation trumped lust. "Why'd you lock us in?" Because she tried hard, her voice only shook a little.

He flashed the key in front of her and dropped it into his pants pocket. "Never know who might wander by. I wanted to make certain we're safe is all." He made a huffing sound. "Most women appreciate that sort of thing."

"No one would come up this trail in the middle of the night."

"Hey, I'm sort of a city boy. We believe in locking the bad guys out." He shrugged. "If you want to hang your jacket, there're hooks by the fire. It looks pretty wet to me."

Alice crossed her arms over her chest and stared at Jed. He stared back. Tension sizzled in the air between them. She held out a hand. "My axe." She gestured to guns on racks along the walls. "Looks as if there are plenty of weapons in here. Besides, my ice axe isn't a weapon, it's a climbing aid."

"Let's just say I'm not enamored of watching my back. Look —" he balanced her ice axe against a wall, stepped away from it, and spread his hands in front of him "—you're apprehensive because you don't know me. How about if I'm feeling the same way?"

She sidled past him and tucked her axe behind her pack where it had been before. "I have no idea how I'm feeling," she muttered, "other than tired."

Jed moved past her to the sink and pumped water into a glass. Crossing the cabin, he handed it to her. "Drink this," he suggested. "Once you're done, let me hang your jacket near the fire where it can dry a little. It's so wet, steam's rising from it."

CHAPTER 2

Earlier That Day

Jeddediah stood off by the side in a cave deep under the Palisade Range in the Sierra Nevada Mountains. Rush torches lined the walls. Stalactites and stalagmites glistened wetly. Some were so large they met in the middle, creating twisted pillars. Clan leader for wolves, Jed watched with pride as his shifter pack comported themselves well against bears, mountain cats, and coyotes.

A number of contests were in progress, requiring both strength and wits. Every gathering closed with games to defray the seriousness—and stress—of hours of discussion. The last challenge, paw to paw combat where the fighters couldn't draw on their magic, was the hardest of all. Usually, the bears won because of their superior bulk and almost impenetrable coats. But this time, it was looking like his wolves just might triumph.

He sidestepped nimbly out of the way as a coyote and mountain cat tumbled by him locked in a flurry of teeth and claws. The contests ran until first blood stained the ground. He and the other three clan leaders were quick to call a fight if it became too destructive. They needed every single shifter. To lose even one in a mock skirmish would be unforgivable.

Jed moved farther from the battling pairs. He needed space to think. The last two days had hosted a special meeting of the clans. Their survival was threatened, and it was time to act. Ancient beyond reckoning, their four shifter groups drew power from the four directions and the four elements. Wolves were west and earth, mountain cats south and fire, coyotes east and air, and bears north and water.

For centuries, each clan kept to themselves. As North America filled with people, shifters migrated west in their search for freedom to roam in animal form. When that didn't work anymore because the western states filled with people, they spent more and more time as humans to disguise their true natures. Soon it became obvious the clans had to work together, or none of them would survive.

Much like their forbearers in Europe, humans in the United States had little tolerance for shifters. After the First World War, things escalated dramatically, maybe because the troops in Europe ran into men who shimmered into other forms and used magic to both kill and protect themselves. Europe was more compact than the States, with fewer places to hide.

Jed snorted. Regardless of the reason, after centuries of near anonymity, shifters had re-entered human consciousness and been labeled a *problem*. Hunters—religious zealots who embraced chastity—came after them in droves.

"Do you think there'll be any of us left to meet next year?" The leader of the bear clan, Keir, sidled over while Jed was lost in thought.

Jed nodded. "Sure, but maybe not a hundred years from now."

Keir shook shaggy black hair away from his weather-beaten face. He was a couple inches taller than Jed and outweighed him by a good fifty pounds. "We must prioritize mating."

"Easier said than done. We have to run free to spur the mating urge. When we're locked in our human forms for weeks and months on end, it mutes…everything."

"I tell you, we should all move to Utah and Arizona. We'd blend right in with the Mormons and their group marriages. Lots of open country too."

Jed blew out a breath. Keir had a point. Shifters formed family groups with two or three males and a female. The male contingent formed first, and then went in search of their mated female. Of late, there were lots of male duos and trios that lacked females to produce the next generation. "Maybe you're right."

"I know I am. Only problem is if we all ended up in the southwestern states, we'd be too visible."

A growl bubbled from Jed's throat. He could almost feel his tail swish back and forth. The urge to shift was irresistible, so he did. He was already naked, so ruined clothes weren't a problem.

Keir joined him. They switched to telepathic speech. *"I may have found a woman,"* he confided.

"Really? One who is willing to join your family group?"

Keir nodded. *"Yes. I explained everything. How she'd become one of us through the mating ritual."* He grunted. *"At first she said she had to think about it. But I wasn't worried. The mate bond snared her. She was so hot she came just rubbing up against me. She stopped by right before we were getting ready to leave."* He chuckled. *"Wanted to do the mating ritual right then. Said she couldn't wait."*

Jed laughed right along with the bear, but then said, *"Chancy to let her leave your side with knowledge that could sink us."*

Keir scratched deep furrows into the cave's floor with his long front claws. *"I had my lieutenants watching her. They would've brought her to me if she turned into a liability. Some of the clan who remained behind are watching her now."* He reared back on his hind legs. *"I'm desperate for a mate for my family group. Willing to take chances I wouldn't have taken a few years ago."*

Jed's heart went out to the bear. He understood because he felt the same way. Hunters had gotten cagy. They knew more about shifters than they ever had in the past. It was entirely possible they knew about their dwindling numbers. Jed had no doubt they'd stoop to anything, including using women as bait. All full-blooded shifters were male. Human females who mated with them absorbed some shifter magic through semen, but not enough to change form.

"Oh, look." Keir dropped to all fours and shoulder butted him. *"We need to go to the judges' table. They're calling the games for this gathering."*

Jed shot Keir a wolfish grin, his tongue lolling. *"Yes, and I do believe we won for a change."*

"Only because it's gotten harder and harder to find places to shift. Some of my guys hardly remember what their animal side feels like."

Keir spoke true, and it made Jed sad and angry by turns. He followed the bear to the judges' station and stood by while the winners were announced, but fury simmered just below the surface. Dropping into his wolf form and killing small rodents muted his rage, at least for a while, but now wasn't the time.

He drew his jaws back into a snarl. They'd lost so much ground, he feared they'd be forced to keep right on hiding until the last of them was Hunted to extinction.

He reached for his human body and trotted to where he'd left his clothes. Dark wool pants, a tan cotton shirt, and a multi-colored woolen jacket lay in a heap. He dressed, pushed his feet into socks and well-worn leather boots, and gathered his two lieutenants. Both had won awards and beamed proudly at him. The other fifty or so wolf shifters who'd attended the gathering milled about. A few of them had mates, but females never came to shifter gatherings.

"Come on." Jed walked up the sloping ramp to the cave's well-hidden entrance. It was still early in the day, not much past mid-morning. He pushed magic out, fanning it about. No one. They'd figured the Sierras would be empty this time of year, and they were. He ducked beneath a low overhang and came out into bright sunlight. Jed shielded his eyes and squinted against the light.

He beckoned to his clan members. "Grab your rifles." He pointed to a group of long guns hidden in the lee of a large boulder. "Until next time."

"Until next time," echoed back to him. The group dispersed, taking off downhill in long, loping strides. Soon only Jed and his two lieutenants were left. Like many shifters, they were a female-less family group.

"Do we really have permission to kill those who Hunt us?" Terin asked. His lips curled in a feral grin. Amber eyes gleamed.

Jed rounded on him. "Only if your life is in imminent danger."

"Okay, okay." Terin held up both hands. "I get that part." A bit shorter than Jed, red hair fell to the middle of his back. All wolf shifters were built the same: tall and rangy with long, lanky limbs and a limber stride.

"I still say it's an improvement," Bron growled. He shoved black hair out of his face. Dark, bottomless eyes masked his feelings.

"Hurry. There's time to chase down some game before the day ends." Jed bounded downhill with an easy lope. He picked his way through talus blocks and around cliffs. Their special cave sat more than a mile from the main trail that wound into the Palisade Basin. The rough terrain provided strong advantages. So far no one had stumbled onto their meeting place.

They could've made better time as wolves, but it was too chancy in broad daylight. If they ran into hunters of any variety, they'd be done for. The common kind would kill them for their pelts. Church-trained Hunters would kill them for their immortal souls.

"I smell a Hunter." Terin careened down the steep slope and caught up to Jed, panting a little.

Jed sniffed the air. He'd been lost in his thoughts again. He needed to mate. The urge was strong now that he'd spent time in his wolf form. He shoved his erection to a more comfortable position and sorted scents. Damn if Terin wasn't right. He slammed a fist against his thigh.

"Good call. I'm ashamed I didn't notice."

Terin eyed the tented front of Jed's trousers and laughed. "Understandable. All that talk of mating at the gathering got to me too. We need to find a woman. It's been too long since we've had someone who liked all of us."

Jed eyed his lieutenant. "What we need is a mate, not casual sex."

"Whatever you say, boss." Terin rubbed his crotch, a wistful look in his eyes.

"Hey!" Jed snapped his fingers in front of Terin. "Enough of that. You fondling yourself isn't helping me focus at all. What about the Hunter?"

"Trail's not all that fresh, but it's not that old, either. I'll bet he traveled by this spot sometime in the last few hours."

Jed narrowed his eyes to slits. "It could be coincidence. Do you think he was after us?"

Terin shook his head. "Nah. Scent track follows the trail. If he'd been after us, he'd have been crawling around up here."

"Not necessarily—"

Bron chugged alongside. "I smell—" he began, but Jed waved him to silence.

"We already know." He sucked in a breath and looked from one to the other of his lieutenants. "There's only one of him and three of us. If we run into him, we're just a bunch of guys out for a spot of early season hunting. If he figures out what we are—and that's likely because they can scent us—we jump him."

"And kill him," Terin snarled.

"Maybe," Jed cautioned. "Wait for my command on that. I know the clans are out for blood, but I can't see where it furthers our cause to engage the enemy in an all-out war. There are way too many of them, and we'd lose."

JED SAT in a wooden chair on the generous front porch that wrapped around Lon Chaney's cabin with his legs splayed in front of him. He rubbed a hand over his pleasantly full stomach. Terin and Bron were out back butchering the remains of the deer and mountain cat they'd killed. There hadn't been any sign of the Hunter they'd scented earlier. Maybe he was going across Jigsaw Pass and out over Bishop Pass. It was a popular route.

His hand strayed lower, stroking himself through his trousers. His cock had been giving him nothing but grief since the up close and personal discussion on mating at the gathering. He shook his head. What a difference a few hundred years made. Before humans decided shifters were a threat, women vied with one another to see who got to have sex with them. The pairing gave a woman power and status.

Not anymore. Mate bond or no, Keir would be lucky if the

woman who said she wanted him didn't turn him in to collect one of the bounties lavishly offered for information about shifters.

His cock jumped against his hand. It didn't give a shit about philosophy. It had liked it a whole lot better when it had a woman's body to bury itself in. He tilted his head and listened with his wolf senses. Terin and Bron chatted while they worked. It was unlikely he'd be disturbed in the few moments it would take to satisfy himself.

Jed unbuttoned his trousers. His cock sprang out, and he closed a hand around it. His other hand toyed with his nipples, tweaking and teasing them, before he lowered it to cup his balls. He stroked his shaft, starting with a soft, tormenting touch. It didn't take long before the feathery strokes turned into the firm rhythm he preferred. His heartbeat sounded loud against his ears. He heard himself make a growling, grunting sound and knew it had been far too long since he'd come. He thought he should be quiet, but then he didn't care. His lieutenants would leave him alone once they figured out what he was doing.

His hand pumped faster as he swelled against his fingers. His hips thrust hard upward, and his head fell back. Bouncing breasts and wet, gleaming pussies half-hidden by curly hair filled his mind. Jed imagined shoving deep inside a woman, taking her from behind. The firm globes of a perfect ass banged against his thighs, and he held onto her hips as he drove himself home inside her. His cock bucked in his hand, and then did it again. Heat spilled through him, setting his nerves on fire. Semen arced and spattered the ground. He stroked himself some more, wondering if he could come again. He was still rock hard. His climax had barely tapped the tip of his lust.

He panted, breath harsh in his throat, and tightened his

grip on his penis. He worked it some more, swirling semen around the sensitive head. He moved the hand cradling his balls back just a little and put pressure on the spot right behind them. *Perfect!* Jed fucked his hand harder and harder until another orgasm roared through him. More intense this time, his cock jerked and spasmed as waves of lust blasted through him.

He lay in a gasping, quivering heap working at getting his breath back.

"I thought I smelled sex."

Jed's eyes snapped open at the sound of Terin's voice. "Show a little respect," he growled.

Terin snorted. "I would, but you've got to pull yourself together. That Hunter is closing on us. Before you ask, it's the same one we smelled earlier."

Jed leapt to his feet. "Tell me." He grabbed an old towel draped over the chair next to his and wiped himself off before stuffing his cock back into his pants and zipping up.

"It's only been the past couple of minutes. Bron smelled it first. There are two people."

Jed narrowed his eyes. "I thought you just said it was the one from this morning. How come we didn't sense the other Hunter earlier?"

Terin shook his head. "Sorry. I wasn't clear. Only one Hunter, but he has a woman with him. They're probably still a couple thousand feet above us, but they're coming right down that mountainside." He pointed across the river.

"It's ridiculously steep and clogged with deadfall. Who the hell would be that stupid?"

Terin shrugged. "Does it matter?"

"I suppose not. Except if they break their damn necks it will mean a hell of a lot of trouble for us. This mountain will be crawling with authority figures and search parties."

Bron trotted around the cabin and glanced at Jed. "We finished packing the meat away. What's next, boss?"

Jed ran options through his mind, grateful for his brief sexual respite. It really helped clear his thoughts. "We stay here doing just what we're doing. Unless he bothers us, we ignore him."

"What about the woman?" Terin asked.

"Same deal. Besides, if she's his girlfriend—" his voice trailed off. Hunters were celibate. They didn't have girlfriends.

"She could be like a sister or something," Bron offered.

Jed made a decision. "We're going to go around back. I don't want him to think we're staring at him. In fact, if we escape his notice, all the better. Maybe we'll get lucky and the pair of them will cross the creek, hit the trail, and head downhill without bothering us at all."

"He'll smell us," Bron protested.

Jed shook his head. "Not if the wind keeps up. It's blowing away from where we are."

"I hope you're wrong." Terin snarled low in the back of his throat. "I want to kill that son of a bitch."

"We all do. Come on." Jed led the way to the far side of the cabin so its thick walls stood between them and the Hunter.

They were pitching horseshoes when the unmistakable sound of a large object crashing through timber snapped Jed's head up. He took off running for the flat, open glade where it was relatively easy to cross the creek. Bron and Terin followed.

"What are we doing?" Terin asked.

"Seeing if whoever fell is dead," Jed called over one shoulder.

"Might've been a boulder," Bron said.

Jed didn't think so. With his wolf senses dialed in, it didn't take long to locate the man's position. It took a while to get to him, though. The mountainside was a forty-five degree slope clotted with thick deadfall. At least the body was below the snowline. Terin got there first. He was hunkered next to a tall, unconscious, red-haired man when Jed climbed up to him.

"Not dead," Terin spat.

"He could be," Bron muttered, panting as he joined the other two.

Jed knelt next to the Hunter and reached out with his shifter magic. The man was deeply unconscious. Jed probed his skull and found a large lump at its base. "Looks like he banged his head on a rock."

"Great. We can leave him here. Since you seem ambivalent about us killing him, the elements will do it for us." Terin pushed to his feet. "Or maybe the local mountain lions."

Jed shook his head. "No. He's too close to the cabin. Last thing we need is the sheriff and coroner and a bunch of their boys around here. Remember, if any of them are Hunters, they'll be able to smell us if they get close."

"We could leave earlier than we planned," Bron suggested.

"Yeah, we could, but I have a better idea. Let's drag him to the cabin and chuck him over a horse. You two can haul him to the truck parked by Glacier Lodge. From there, it'll be easy enough to drive him to the hospital in Bishop. That way we come off as good Samaritans, and if bozo—" Jed thwacked the unconscious man with the back of his hand "—starts raving about smelling shifters up here, no one will suspect it was us."

A faint cry caught Jed's wolf senses.

"Brent. Brent."

The woman.

He'd forgotten about her. Judging from the sound of things, she was still a long way up the mountain. He traded gazes with his lieutenants.

"Yeah, we hear her too," Bron muttered. "Let's get moving. We can deal with her later."

"Sure. She'll thank us for getting her brother—or whoever he is—to medical care," Terin said.

"Each of you take an arm," Jed instructed. "I'll get below you, and you can lower him to me. We've got gravity on our side. It shouldn't take all that long."

〜

IT TOOK LONGER than Jed anticipated, though. Lots longer. The man, Brent, was heavy, maybe two hundred pounds. They'd dropped him a time or two, but hadn't managed to kill him. Jed breathed a sigh of relief once the Hunter was bundled across a horse and on his way down the trail with Terin and Bron riding beside him.

Jed glanced at himself. His clothing was splattered with gore. The Hunter's hands had scraped over rocks and sharp branches. They'd been slick with blood before the three of them managed to maneuver him off the mountainside. Jed's pants were soaked to the thighs. It had been impossible to balance on rocks crossing the creek, so they'd waded, burden suspended between them.

Jed sighed and set his jaw in a firm line. Killing the Hunter had been tempting, but their current plan was better. He'd lived long enough to know killing never solved anything. He shucked his clothes and rinsed them in the creek before draping them over the wooden railing that spanned the front porch. He'd move them inside once he got a fire going.

He scented the air, rich with the scents of small rodents emerging from their dens. It had been dark for a while. Time to hunt and be hunted. He ducked inside and pulled on fresh wool trousers, a blue sweater, and a gray, boiled wool jacket. He focused his shifter magic on sticks of wood in the massive, stone fireplace. Once they caught, he fed larger pieces until he had a respectable blaze going. The heat felt good.

Even from inside the cabin, the woman's scent grew stronger as she worked her way down the mountainside. He'd had to hold himself back, every instinct on edge. Maybe because he'd indulged himself earlier, her bouquet was intoxicating. Musk and wildflowers and something unique and womanly bombarded his enhanced sense of smell. She was right across the river, had been there for maybe half an hour. He'd heard the subtle sounds of her settling in to rest.

Time for him to slip back outside, into the darkness. He wanted to be there when she got close enough to talk with. He wasn't sure what he'd do if she bedded down across the creek. It would be hard to come up with an excuse for disturbing her camp.

I'll come up with something.

His cock had been hard for the last half hour. It was a long time since he'd been this aroused by a human woman. Maybe that meant she was slated to be a shifter mate. Bron and Terin would be delighted. They'd all been lonely. What a delight it would be to welcome her as the one who'd complete their family group…

Stop! What am I going to do, tie her up and hang onto her until she capitulates?

If that's what it takes, a pragmatic inner voice answered.

Shut up. She has to want me as much as I want her—and accept the mate bond. Otherwise, she'll bide her time, escape, and bring the hordes of Hell down on us.

Jed shuttered his thoughts as he slipped outside and took a position in the shadowed recesses of a grove of pine trees. He was desperately lonesome. Had been for years, but that didn't excuse pretending. Either the mate bond would be there. Or it wouldn't. It was never a one-sided affair. If the mate bond was present, she'd want him as much as he wanted her. Of course, it would be difficult for her to accept it, no matter how much she lusted after him. Most humans were programmed to see shifters as one step up from monsters.

By the time he heard the woman slog across the creek, he'd formed a rough plan. He'd charm the socks off her to keep her by his side long enough for her to accept the mate bond—if it was there. He'd know almost instantly, but it would take far longer to ease her into the idea. Jed flexed his fingers. Excitement raced through him. If her scent was any indication...

If there's no bond, I'll send her on her way. No point in indulging myself in a fling, no matter how good she smells.

Part of his magic was telepathic suggestion. It was how shifters managed to elude Hunters some of the time. He'd have to tread softly. She had to come to him of her own accord, not because he pushed in any way. And he'd have to tell her about what he was before anything happened. She was a virgin. He'd determined that by smell.

Not for much longer.

Jed hoped he wasn't deluding himself about the mate bond. He wiped a broad grin off his face, aiming for a return of rational thought, but clear-headedness fled as soon as he pictured the woman, imagining what she might look like. Once she'd had him, of course she'd want Terin and Bron. After all, they were a package deal... The mate bond magic would make her want them just as much as she wanted him.

Stop! I'm getting way, way ahead of myself. I don't even know for sure yet if the bond is there.

Jed couldn't rein in his hope, though. It burned like a beacon in his mind. He considered how to tell her he was a shifter. It would be so much easier if he could bed her first, but the rules were excruciatingly clear. The human female had to know ahead of time what she was getting into. Once he'd had sex with her, she wouldn't be able to keep her hands off him. It wasn't fair if the woman's mind and body weren't in full agreement.

"Sweetheart, there's something I need to tell you," Jed murmured. "Everything you've heard about shifters isn't really true—" He shook his head. No, too defensive. He tried a few other tacks, but wasn't satisfied with any of them.

Hold up, buddy. He chided himself again. *I need to wait until I lay eyes on her and am sure before I plan how to convince her to stay.*

He held himself in check, waiting until she made a less-than-stealthy circuit of the cabin before he approached. Even though he knew her sex beyond any doubt, he called out, "Hey there. You. Show yourself, man," to make her feel they were more evenly matched—both being men and all.

She was so tall, anyone could've made that mistake. Jed was certain it had happened to her before. He was good at manipulating subtleties. Even so, his mouth was dry. Something about the cautious way she'd worked her way around the cabin told him he didn't have any margin for error. If he spooked her, she'd flee.

She was his mated one. Now that she was only a few feet away, he knew it without a shadow of a doubt. His cock knew it too, achingly hard and straining against his trousers. No matter how much he wanted her, he wouldn't run her down and hold her against her will. He had to take this slow and help her trust him. His heartbeat pounded against his ears. This wasn't going to be easy. He wanted to wrap his arms around her and crush her against his body.

"Why should I?" She spun to face him, and he saw her clearly in the beam from his flashlight.

Even exhausted, she was stunning, with high cheekbones and tip-tilted green eyes. Cat eyes. Bulky clothing hid the lines of her body, but he could imagine the swell of breasts pushed against the front of her jacket and lush hips flared below a slender waist. Strands of long, dark hair fell around her face. The rest was gathered behind her. He wondered how long it was. She brandished an ice axe at him, her eyes glittering dangerously.

Good, this one has spirit. She'll need it to accept the mate bond.

"What? You're a woman?" He stepped closer and imbued his words with surprise.

She grasped her ice axe in both hands, holding it in front of her. "Yeah. So what? Leave me alone," she grunted through clenched teeth. "I'm tired and my friend is…lost."

"You don't have to be afraid of me." He extended both hands.

"Why the hell not?"

Jed offered her credit. She sounded furious, and her voice didn't tremble at all. If he hadn't had wolf senses to hand, he'd never have known how scared she was.

"Never mind my questions." She jerked her chin upward. "Get out of my way. I'm headed for the far side of the trail, now I've finally located it."

"Please." He dropped his hands back to his sides. "I won't hurt you. You look exhausted, cold. I know it's good trail back to Glacier Lodge, but it's the middle of the night. Surely morning would be a better bet for travel. After you've rested." He inhaled shallowly and sent a small net of shifter persuasion after his words. "Put your axe down, sweetheart. I'm not going to hurt you."

She shook her head, trying to look tough, but weariness poured from her in waves, and his heart ached for her.

"Go back inside," she said. "You can see I'm not any kind of threat. I'm not going to the lodge. I would, except I need to be in this area at first light to hunt for my friend. Late as it is, it doesn't make sense to do the round trip to Glacier Lodge and back."

Jed cocked his head to one side and called on whatever god watched out for actors to help him pull this off. "Big guy with red hair?"

The woman bit her lower lip and gazed mutely at him, pleading in her eyes.

"Look, I think he'll be okay. We were out hunting and heard something falling. Thought it was the deer we'd shot at. Turned out to be your friend—"

"Awk! You shot Brent!"

Jed waved his hands in front of him. "Calm down, woman. Christ, you're strung tighter than a fiddle. Take a couple of deep breaths. No, we didn't shoot him. Your friend was unconscious because he hit his head on a rock, so we carried him back here. My two buddies took the horses and hauled him down to the lodge. From there, they'll take him to the hospital in Bishop."

She nodded once, sharply. "I need to get moving then. I can drive to the hospital and meet them. If not tonight, then first thing in the morning."

The man held out a hand. "I'm Jed. Jed Starnes. You look beat. There're mountain cats on the prowl. Shot one a few hours ago. They get worse at night. More aggressive. You got a gun?"

She shook her head and ignored his outstretched hand.

Jed did his damnedest to look harmless, non-threatening. "Handshake or no, I have a nice warm fire going inside. You look wet clear through. Nothing you can do tonight, anyway. Get a few shots of Irish whiskey in you, a little soup, and some sleep. Come morning, you can go after your friend."

She kept her ice axe poised. "How'd you get access to Lon Chaney's cabin?"

Jed threw back his head and laughed at the unexpected question. "That's easy. Ever since Chaney senior died in nineteen-thirty, his son's been letting some of us who work with him have the keys. Damn shame the old man died right after he got this place built. It's a beauty. You really should take a look inside."

She blew out a ragged breath. "What is it you do?"

"I'm a production manager for Paramount."

"I thought they were in receivership."

"We are. But we're still making movies."

She slowly dropped her hands.

Relief she wasn't going to bolt sluiced through him. "That's better, sweetheart," he crooned. "Follow me. I promise I don't bite."

"Okay, I guess so. As soon as I've had a bite to eat and dried out a little, I'll bed down on the porch. Not inside with you." She slitted her green eyes his way, waiting for his response.

Jed's tight muscles relaxed. She wasn't going to make this easy, but one step at a time. "Whatever makes you comfortable, sweetheart."

"So long as we're both clear about that."

"We are."

"Oh yeah. Stop calling me sweetheart."

"Fine." He smothered a smile. "What's your name?"

"Alice. I'm Alice." She finally lowered her ice axe.

When he gestured, she walked in front of him into the cabin.

Jed waited until she was inside and putting her things down before he turned the lock and pocketed the key. In case she had a change of heart, he wanted the extra few minutes that locked door would buy him to convince her to stay.

<h1 style="text-align:center">CHAPTER 3</h1>

Alice sputtered and shifted her weight from foot to foot. She never had sat down. They'd began well enough with Jed telling her about Lon Chaney, but then they'd moved to a discussion about Brent. She felt guilty enough about not trying harder to locate him earlier, but the brush-choked slope had been impossible—and then it got dark.

"What is he?" Jed asked softly. "Your husband?"

She gritted her teeth. "No."

"What then? Brother, cousin—"

"He's just a friend, and it's really none of your business. If you'll unlock the door, I'll take my chances with the mountain lions." Alice turned away from him and grabbed her lantern. She slung her pack over one aching shoulder, wincing as its weight dragged on what had to be bruised flesh. Detouring to pick up her ice axe, she strode toward the door, eying the windows as possible escape routes. They could work. She'd have to unlatch the wooden shutters, but still…

Jed moved in front of her and shot her a blinding smile, his eyes glowing like exotic gemstones. She blinked. Alice had

33

never seen such a gorgeous man. Red-gold hair fell to his shoulders. His face was more than handsome. He had a high, broad forehead and sharply cast cheekbones. His teeth were very white and very straight. What would it feel like to run her fingers through that wonderful hair, to stroke his tanned skin?

She shook herself mentally.

What's wrong with me? I have to get out of here.

Alice covered the remaining distance to the door and rattled the knob. "Let me out. It's against the law to hold people against their will."

"You're being hasty. I apologize for discussing your friend."

"Why'd you assume it was a him?"

Jed rolled his eyes. "Because you're the first woman I've ever met who appears to enjoy mountaineering."

She turned and sent a rueful grin skittering across the air between them. "Caught me dead to rights on that one."

He gestured toward a carved wooden sofa with colorful cushions in front of the fireplace. "I'm not being a very good host. Please. Have a seat. Let me get you a drink."

"I don't think so." She curled her fingers around her pack straps and the ice axe's handle. A spicy, exotic scent filled her nostrils. It seemed to be coming from him. A cross between bay rum and musk made her nose twitch. Alice tried to cling to fear and outrage, but felt them slipping away. She took a step closer to him before she realized what she was doing and fixed her gaze on his lips. She wanted to feel them pressed against hers, needed to lose herself in his arms.

How could I be so attracted to him? He's a stranger.

She struggled to regain her equanimity, but her body had other ideas. Against her better judgement, she glanced lower. When she realized she was staring at his crotch, she got hold of herself. Heat flooded her face. She hoped he hadn't noticed the direction of her gaze.

"Please," he repeated and extended a hand. "Alice. Like I said, I haven't been much of a host."

She swallowed hard. It didn't make sense, but she wanted to run into his arms and wrap hers around his strongly-muscled frame to see what it would feel like right up against her. Her nipples hardened, and breath caught in her throat. It was like he was making love to her from ten feet away. For one wild moment, she wanted to strip her clothes off and…

"Here." He walked to her and pried the axe and lantern out of her hands. She tried to hang onto them, but her fingers wouldn't cooperate. Close like that, his lush scent surrounded her. She closed her eyes and inhaled deeply. He tugged her pack off the shoulder it was perched on and set it on the floor.

Christ! For the first time she understood the phrase *it smelled good enough to eat.* To her horror, she parted her lips and turned them upward, as if she were waiting for a lover to kiss her.

What the hell is happening to me?

She shook her head hard enough to rattle her teeth and took a few steps away from him and her pack. She couldn't think. Hell, she could barely breathe. Her crotch was wet, and the center of her sensation throbbed with need.

"What's your last name, Alice?" He moved her pack next to a chair and glided to her side.

"Carey." Her throat was so thick, it was hard to talk.

He slid her wet jacket off her shoulders and draped it over a chair. "Well, Alice Carey, how about if you sit by the fire, and I'll bring you something to drink. Food too, if you want. Your boots look pretty wet. Maybe you'd like to take them off."

She tried to tell him that no, she needed to leave, but the words wouldn't come. A part of her—the wise part—wanted to run like hell. The rest of her couldn't have left if someone lit a firecracker under her ass. She breathed in his scent. It was like a balm, heating her nerve endings and soothing her fears at the same time.

She watched his graceful form move to the kitchen alcove. He had a high, tight ass and long legs. She wondered again what his skin would feel like beneath her fingers. Alice caught a glimpse of herself in a mirror mounted to one side of the fireplace. Spots of color rode high on both cheeks. Her eyes glowed. Her nipples were fully visible pressed against the fabric of her wool shirt, so were the curves of her breasts. She bit her lower lip and chastised herself for not wearing a bra. She'd hoped Brent might get...ideas if he could see more of her body. Except she flaunted it right and left, and he never did.

And now here she was with a stranger—

Am I so desperate I don't care anymore, just so long as someone has sex with me?

It didn't feel like that, though. Not really. It was more like she'd known Jed in another lifetime and had some sort of bond to him. Alice rolled her mental eyes.

I'm being ridiculous. It's just nerves and exhaustion catching up.

"Here you go, sweetheart." Jed pressed a glass into her hand and set a plate on the coffee table near the fireplace. "Come on. Sit. You must be exhausted."

Alice sat, but it was because her legs didn't want to hold her up anymore. To her surprise, he knelt and unlaced her boots. Once both layers were loosened, he tugged first one, and then the other off.

"Just as I thought," he murmured. "Your socks are soaked." He stripped them gently off her feet and hung them over the table's edge nearest the fire.

It did feel good to get her heavy boots off. Alice wriggled her toes. They were cold. Almost as if Jed could read her thoughts, he rubbed her feet between remarkably warm hands. She lounged back against the cushions, luxuriating in the touch of his fingertips on her chilled flesh. Remembering the glass in her hand, she took a sip of whiskey. It burned all the way to her stomach, but felt so invigorating, she followed it with another. Her free hand moved with a will of its own. She yanked it back before it buried itself in Jed's shiny hair.

He pushed back on his heels and rose in a single, fluid motion. In moments he was back. Kneeling by her feet, he wrapped a warm towel around them.

She moaned softly, delighted by being pampered. "Where'd you get a hot towel? Surely you don't have electricity all the way out here."

He laughed. "It was on a hook by the fireplace. The fire warms the stones, so anything hanging next to them gets toasty." He latched his incredible blue eyes onto hers. "Relax. Everything will be all right. Have a bit more whiskey. It's from Ireland and more than twenty-five years old. There's bread and cheese on the table." He winked at her, a slow, lascivious gesture that made her heart beat faster. "Let me spoil you a little."

"I really shouldn't." Her words lacked conviction. She knew it. Worse, so did he.

He rubbed her feet through the towel, then wrapped it around one while taking the other in his hands. He massaged her weary arches and the ball of her foot with knowing fingers. "Do you always do what you should?"

The sexual innuendo was unmistakable. Her swollen pussy lips and clit thrummed with tension. She took another sip of whiskey, letting it roll around on her tongue. Rich and oaky, it tasted like liquid gold. "Usually."

"What's that saying? Good girls never have any fun." He worked her toes, and then shifted to the top of her foot and her ankle.

"I climb mountains. Most girls don't do that." Her head buzzed pleasantly from the liquor.

I should eat something. If I don't, I'll be drunk in no time.

Alice leaned forward and took a slice of cheese from the blue earthenware plate on the table in front of her. She wrapped a piece of bread around it and took a bite. The bread was flaky and fresh. It tasted homemade.

The longer he worked on her feet, the more she wanted him. Alice felt mystified. She'd masturbated her lust away before, but what was happening now existed in a whole different league. She'd never felt she'd die if she didn't come. It didn't take much to imagine those strong hands moving up her calves, settling between her legs, and... Her hips twitched. She covered the involuntary motion by shifting her position on the couch.

"I was talking about fun, not mountaineering." He rubbed the spaces between her toes with gentle strokes.

"But they're the same." Her face heated again. The special place deep inside her ached to be filled. She wished she knew more about sex. It wasn't the sort of thing people ever talked about, though. She'd hunted down medical texts in the library, but they hadn't been terribly helpful.

"There's more than one way to have fun." Jed wrapped the foot he'd been working on in the towel and switched back to the other. "Is the towel still warm enough, sweetheart? Would you like me to get another?"

"No, really, I'm fine." Alice was flustered—and so aroused she couldn't think. She rubbed her thighs together. Maybe there'd be some way she could sneak off to the privy. Her head would be clearer if she made herself come. She drank more whiskey. Between that and his suggestive comments about good girls and fun, the nub between her legs pulsed mercilessly.

She settled into the feel of his hands on her flesh. Her feet really were tired. The heavy, two-layer mountaineering boots didn't have much give to them. They were made by a German manufacturer, and the standing joke in the climbing community was you had to adapt to them because they'd never bow to you. The next time she raised her glass, she was surprised to find it empty. Alice set it on the table and leaned back against the cushions.

"Would you like more?" His voice was rich and smooth, just like the whiskey.

She shook her head. "I've probably had more than enough. I —" Alice stifled a gasp.

He'd bent his head and taken her big toe in his mouth. He sucked gently, and then ran his tongue down the underside of her foot. Her hips writhed against the sofa cushions. His mouth moved to her second toe. He sucked harder, and then ran a nail down the underside of her foot.

Heat roared through Alice. Her arousal from moments before was nothing compared with what was happening to her now. Her thighs fell open. Fingers moved between her legs. Momentarily confused, she was horrified to discover she'd jammed a hand atop her vulva and was rubbing her clit through layers of pants. She tried to drag her hand away, but her body had other ideas. It wanted to come. Had to have release or she'd die.

Her face heated with lust and humiliation. She glanced at him. One of his hands was buried in his crotch. The swell of an erection tantalized her and made her even hotter.

He must've sensed her gaze on him because he raised his attention from her foot. "Just let it happen, sweetheart," he murmured, his voice raspy with passion. "We needed to start somewhere. If you were any closer to coming, you'd be there. Go on, rub yourself. Or—" something feral and untamed blazed from the depths of his blue eyes "—I can do it for you."

He moved his hand from his cock and placed it atop hers. Slowly at first, then faster, she showed him what she needed. The added weight of his hand and the heat of his body undid her. Breath hitched in her throat, and her heart thudded hard. She closed her free hand over a nipple and pinched the puckery tip. Capturing it with two fingers, she twirled it as sensation escalated between her legs. Her hips bucked against the combined pressure of their hands, and bucked again. She barely recognized the long, low shriek that filled the room as hers. Waves of climax pounded through her, and she just kept coming.

He rubbed her until her hips quieted. Alice tugged her hand from under his and buried her face in it. Shame filled her. Jed was a stranger. She'd just masturbated herself to orgasm in front of him.

"I—I'm not usually like this." Her voice ran down. She didn't know what to say. All loose women probably proclaimed their innocence.

The sofa shifted as he settled next to her. He draped an arm around her shoulders and pulled her against his body. "It's nothing to be ashamed of. I know you're a virgin, and I'm the first man who's ever touched you."

"How could you possibly know that?" Her voice was muffled against his shoulder.

"That's part of a talk we need to have. But I want you to get some sleep first. Come on. There's a bed behind the curtain. Let me tuck you in. We'll talk after you wake." He got to his feet and extended both hands. She took them and let him draw her into an embrace. The jut of his erection pressed against her stomach.

Feeling bold, she reached between them and curled her

fingers around it. "Would you like—I mean, uh, you helped me, so..." Alice didn't have the first idea how to make a man come, but she was sure she could figure it out. The idea thrilled her and made sparks ignite between her legs again. That she wanted more from Jed mystified her. She'd just come. Why wasn't she satisfied? She'd read about nymphomaniacs.

Oh my God. Is that what I'm turning into?

Instead of letting go, she tightened her fingers around him. Heat from his body nearly scalded her through the fabric of his trousers.

He cut her words off with a kiss, teasing her lips and tongue with his own. He tasted sweet, like the whiskey, and she lost herself in the wonderful feel of his firm lips on hers. His cock jerked against her hand where she still held it. She'd never touched a man's penis before. The rigid length of him fascinated her and made her hotter than hell.

When he raised his head, he said, "Yes, I want you to do all those things to me, but first you need to sleep. Come on." He placed an arm around her and led her through the curtain. The bedroom was illuminated by a candle burning in a glass holder. A double four-poster bed with a patchwork quilt tossed over it sat in one corner. A matching mirrored dresser was off to one side. Both pieces were richly carved dark wood. True to his word, Jed turned back the coverlet and tucked her under it. He bent and kissed her forehead, then turned to leave.

"Aren't you going to sleep with me? Er, I meant, get some sleep." A fresh wave of embarrassment filled her. She was acting like a whore. Well-bred women didn't talk about sex, not directly, anyway. They waited for men to do the asking—for pretty much everything.

He laughed and blew out the candle. "I'll be in front of the fire. Just call if you need me. If I lie down you'll never get the rest you need." The last thing she heard before she fell asleep was the clump of his footsteps moving through the cabin.

∼

JED TOSSED another piece of wood on the fire. His cock raged against the front of his pants, but he ignored it. He wanted to hold onto a sexual edge, not dilute it by jacking off. The corners of his mouth curved into a lusty grin. What a hot little number Alice was. Better than his wildest dreams. When she shoved her hand between her legs, he'd wanted to crow his delight. That she hadn't even realized what she was doing was even better. The mate bond held her in thrall. Between that and her latent sexuality, he could stoke her passion into a blazing fire. She'd come twice with his hand atop hers, one peak piled right after the next. He wondered if she understood what a gift that was.

He imagined what she'd look like without clothes. He'd pretty much seen her breasts through the fabric of her long underwear top and thought it odd she wasn't wearing some sort of brassiere. Jed nodded to himself. The lack of underwear wasn't such a puzzle after all. She'd called Brent a friend, but he'd seen longing for the Hunter in her mind. No bra meant she hadn't given up trying to seduce him.

I'll have to disabuse her of that notion. And damned quick. She has no idea what he is—or that his kind take vows of celibacy before they're accepted into the Hunter ranks. Bastards whose sole mission in life is to search out and kill shifters.

He lifted his upper lip in a snarl and felt his canines lengthen before he got his fury under control.

His thoughts returned to Alice's wonderful body and her magnificent, waist-length hair. Thick and lush, he couldn't wait to undo her braid and bury his fingers in it. She had delightfully long legs. They had to be well-muscled for her to do the things she did in the mountains. He pictured them locked around his hips and his cock buried deep inside her body.

Jed laughed to himself. Alice wasn't the only one in thrall to the mate bond. It poured through him like well-aged wine: tantalizing and compelling. His breath quickened. His hand drifted to his hard on, but he jerked it away. Getting to his feet, he paced from one end of the cabin to the other to get blood moving to something other than his penis.

He blew out a breath. He'd cheated—but only a little. When she'd gotten up and huffed her way to the door—scared, but full of bravado—he'd called up a bit of shifter magic and soothed her fears. He'd done it outside too. Both times had been unconscious because he couldn't stand to see her frightened or suffering. The mate bond was weaving its magic, and he already felt fiercely protective of his new mate. Nothing would ever harm her, not while he had anything to say about it.

Jed stared into the fire, thinking about the next day. He couldn't use magic when he explained what he was to her. It was against the rules. She had to accept him on her own, or he'd need to obliterate her memory of him and let her go. Much as he wanted a mate, his obligation as alpha to the Wolf Clan came first.

The way Keir, the Bear Clan alpha, had handled things was foolish. Too much margin for error to give the woman information and let her out of his sight. Jed thought about his counterpart, and said a quick prayer for his safety and that of his fellow shifters.

He considered what to tell Alice—and in which order. First, he needed to clarify what Brent was. Jed had a sneaking hunch it would come as a relief once she understood her erstwhile friend had ignored her charms because of what he considered a higher calling.

Describing what he was would be much harder. Humans held preconceived notions about shifters—lots of them. She'd be horrified at first. Jed tossed one more log on the fire, damped the flue, and sat down. He steepled his fingers together and rested his chin atop them. Maybe it would be better to get her talking about herself. He'd taken a peek inside her mind, so he already knew a great deal, but if he could get her to confide in him, it might relax her.

He didn't have to pretend to be interested in her. Linked by the mate bond, he was so taken, it was a struggle not to stride to the bed, join her, and fuck her until she couldn't walk. Jed gritted his teeth. Once wakened through the bond, the mating urge was strong. So strong, it had been known to make shifters physically ill if denied.

Can't make love with her, he scolded himself. *Not yet.*

She had to know what he was, first. He had to tell her about the mate bond too. Having sex with him would change her irrevocably. She'd get some of his shifter magic. Once mated, she'd want him with a strength and ferocity to equal his own. No way to wipe that out of her mind with magic. No, she needed to make this choice of her own free will and with a clear head.

He'd have to tell her about his lieutenants, Terin and Bron, too. Shifter marriages were group affairs, but not on paper. In the eyes of the world, she'd be married to Jed, and Jed alone, but the four of them would form a family group. His jaw tightened, and he forced himself to relax. It would be a lot for Alice to take in. He hoped to hell she was up to it.

He'd sensed her exhaustion. It was one of the main reasons he insisted she get some sleep. After all, from what she'd told him, she'd been on the move since the middle of the previous night.

"That's it," he muttered as he watched the flames sputter and spark against one another. "I'll encourage her to tell me about her life—all of it. Even her parents' deaths that I saw in her mind. Once her story is out on the table, I'll tell her I'm a shifter. If she doesn't back away shrieking, I'll work in the mate bond and the rest of it, but gradually."

Telling her about Bron and Terin would have to wait. She might take the information better once she wasn't a virgin anymore.

Jed's hand strayed to his erection, and he stroked himself through his trousers. Once she'd accepted his shifter status and what fucking him would mean, they'd take a sex break. To celebrate. His cock twitched against his hand. It wanted Alice. Wanted to bury itself deep in the hot warmth of her body and consummate the mate bond.

Soon, he patted himself. *She'll be ours soon enough. I hope.*

All the things that could potentially blow up in his face marched through his mind, but he pushed them aside. No point borrowing trouble. Two hours ago, having Alice in the cabin, let alone sleeping in his bed, seemed like anything but a sure bet. He'd always been lucky, though, and tomorrow fortune would gift him with her grace.

He was certain of it. Telling her about Terin and Bron would unfold easily, naturally, once they'd had sex.

Aw Jesus, hope to hell I'm right about that.

If he wasn't, making love with him would damn near ruin her life—and his. He'd long for her forever, and she'd never be able to love anyone but him.

CHAPTER 4

lice rolled over and opened her eyes. The gray light of early morning filtered through heavy drapes because they weren't fully drawn. She felt disoriented for a moment, and then memory of the previous night hit her between the eyes. She groaned.

I've got to get out of here.

She had no idea what Jed had in mind. For all she knew, he planned to keep her as some sort of latter day sex slave. Her pussy thought that was a grand idea, but she told it to go pound sand. Just thinking about Jed made her clit pulse with need. She moved her fingers to her nipples. They were already peaked. She rubbed them through her top, and then lowered a hand between her legs.

What the fuck am I doing?

She jerked her hand back and worried something had gone badly wrong the previous night. Was she one of those women who, once she succumbed to sex with a man, was worthless for anything else? She'd never believed the whispered tales, but she seemed to be living proof they were true.

She eyed the window. It looked as if it would open. Maybe she could dress quietly and just sneak away. She'd miss some of the things in her rucksack, but her car keys were in her pants pocket. They were all she really needed.

Wrong. My boots. I need my boots.

She clamped her teeth together. Chances of creeping past Jed to grab her boots sitting next to the fireplace were slim to none. She scanned the room. Several pairs of shoes were lined up beneath a dresser. She had big feet: men's size eleven. Maybe luck would be with her. Alice crept from the bed. If she weren't trying for silence, she would've grunted in pain. Every muscle ached from yesterday's climb. She'd almost made it to the shoes when Jed shoved the curtain aside.

"Good morning, sweetheart," he said breezily. "There's a chamber pot under the bed if you need it. Come on out when you're ready. I just started some coffee. How do you like your eggs?"

Alice swallowed hard. She squared her shoulders and turned to Jed. "Um, look. Last night was a big mistake. I was tired and drunk. What I plan to do this morning is get dressed and leave." Nails dug into her palm when she fisted her hands. "You will let me leave."

Something flitted across his face, but she couldn't make it out in the dim light. "Of course I'll let you leave, but first we need to talk. I told you that last night."

She lifted her chin. "What if I don't want to talk?"

He exhaled sharply. "Unfortunately, that's not one of your choices." She opened her mouth, but he waved her to silence. "If you still want to leave once we're done with our conversation, I won't try to stop you. I give you my word." He held out a hand.

She ignored it. Anger set her nerves on edge. "Fine. Get out of here. I'll be out presently."

The curtain fell back into place. Alice fumed. She dragged the porcelain bowl from under the bed, squatted, and peed.

How fucking convenient, an inner voice snarked. *This way he didn't have to let me go outside to use the privy.*

Her mood didn't improve when urine sloshed over the top wetting her bare feet. She wiped them with a towel hanging from a hook near the door. Not much more she could do without water.

She'd slept in her clothes, so getting dressed was a non-issue. She covered the chamber pot and pushed it back under the bed, tugged the quilt into place, and stomped into the front room. Jed's back was to her. He was busy over a kerosene-powered camp stove.

"You really should have the door open when you use that," she snapped. "Unless you want to asphyxiate both of us."

His back stiffened, but he didn't turn around. When he spoke, his tone was mild. "I did open the window at this end of the cabin. It's what I usually do when I cook in here, and I'm still alive. Coffee's ready. I didn't know how you—"

"Never mind. I'll make my own." She gathered her socks and her boots and sat in a chair to put them on. The smell of bacon and eggs frying filled the cabin. Her stomach growled. Alice shut her eyes for a moment and gathered her thoughts. She wasn't really frightened anymore. If he'd wanted to kill her, she'd be dead. Part of her was still furious, though. Jed hadn't said as much, but he was holding her prisoner.

Another part of her wanted more of what he'd dished out the previous night. Her pussy was wet and swollen with need. It ached. So did her breasts. She watched him sidelong, grudgingly appreciating his skill in the kitchen. Most men, other than chefs, couldn't boil water.

"About ready to eat?" he asked.

She nodded, but then realized he couldn't see her. "Yeah."

She got up and walked briskly to his side. His wonderful scent enveloped her, trumping the odor of food. Alice batted back an insane desire to throw her arms around him. She pushed her tongue against her teeth. There was definitely something wrong—with her. She hoped it would fix itself once she left Jed and the cabin behind. To divert herself from the sexual images tumbling through her mind, she grabbed a metal mug and poured coffee into it. "Is there any milk?"

"In the cold box under the window."

By the time she returned with it, he'd dished up two plates and set them on the well-worn kitchen table. Alice poured milk into her coffee and sipped it. A few grounds, but not bad. She smiled her thanks, then remembered she was angry with him and looked away.

He snorted. "For a minute there, you forgot yourself. I could've sworn you were about to thank me."

She pulled out a chair and sat. Once she started shoveling food into her mouth, she didn't stop. It was thirty hours since she'd had a decent meal. Alice glanced up to find his gaze settled on her.

"You ate as if you were starving, sweetheart. Can I make you some more?"

Alice's cheeks heated. Despite her resolve to remain angry, her lips parted in a shy smile. "Could you? If it's too much trouble, I can scramble up a couple more eggs. Is there any more of the bread we had last night?"

"How about this?" He got to his feet. "I'll make us more eggs. You can toast some bread over the fire. The grate's hanging next to the fireplace."

Alice dug through the sack he pointed to and got the rest of a loaf of bread. She sliced it and went to get the long handled grate. "I'm surprised you trusted me with a knife."

He laughed. The sound was mellow, and it warmed her. "I

wasn't worried. You're angry with me, but I don't think you'd hurt me."

"Does that mean I can pick up my ice axe without you pitching a fit?" She flipped the grate to toast the other side of the bread.

"You can do whatever you want with it, sweetheart. And I meant what I said about you being free to leave—once we've talked."

Something about his tone was so sincere, the place that had been wound tight as a spring inside her relaxed a little. "Do we have butter?" She opened the grate and removed the toast. It was hot enough, she laid it on her sleeve to carry back to the kitchen.

"Yup. Honey too." He laid both on the table, along with their plates piled high with more eggs. "Sorry, we ran out of bacon. I could cook up some venison or mountain lion—"

"That's okay." She tucked into the food.

When their plates were empty, and she'd worked her way through her second cup of coffee, he reached across the table and placed a hand over hers. "There are some things you need to know," he began and cleared his throat, "about your friend."

She frowned. "What? Did you lie to me last night?"

He shook his head. "No, nothing like that. He really did hit his head on a rock and my two buddies really did take him to the hospital in Bishop."

"What then? You didn't know Brent, so what could you possibly tell me about him?"

"Did you know he's a Hunter?"

She knitted her brows together. "What kind of question is that? Of course he hunts. Most men do."

Jed shook his head again. "Not that kind of hunter." He sucked in a breath. "You're an attractive woman, Alice. Didn't you ever wonder why he never so much as kissed you?"

How can he know that?

A chill marched up her spine.

"I know that," he said without missing a beat, "because I know what he is."

The chill deepened into a shudder. "Y-you can read my mind?"

"Yes. That and other things. Brent hunts shifters. He traded a normal life for one of celibacy and obedience. It's why he's never touched you."

She slumped against the back of her chair, stunned. Puzzle pieces clicked into place. The odd telephone calls where Brent would race out the door, leaving a half-touched supper. His reluctance to allow her into his life in more than a peripheral fashion. His encouragement for her to find someone who was free. She'd never understand why he wasn't. Until now.

"Oh." She took a shallow breath. "Why didn't he tell me?"

"He couldn't. Secrecy is part of his vows."

Jed tightened his hand over hers. She thought about pushing it away, but didn't. His skin felt good, warm and comforting.

"How do you know these things?" Alice wasn't sure she wanted to hear the answer.

"I'll tell you, but first, I want to know more about you."

"Huh?"

"Tell me about who you are, Alice. Your family. What's important to you?"

"Why?"

"Because I'm interested."

She bit her lip. "You can read my mind. Doesn't that mean you can just go in and get whatever information you want?"

"It doesn't work quite like that. Come on, Alice. Don't make this hard. Look at me."

She lifted her gaze to his. Yearning blazed hot in the depths of his blue eyes. It didn't make sense. She chewed on her lower lip, thinking. "You couldn't possibly be that interested. You don't have any idea who I am."

He smiled. It lit his face from the inside out. "Ah, but you're wrong, sweetheart. Go ahead, tell me about you."

Alice nodded to herself. Her story was simple enough. It wouldn't take long. "My parents died when I was sixteen. Dad got the flu; Mom had cancer. Within six months of one another, they were just gone. I didn't have any brothers or sisters. All my aunts and uncles lived clear across the country. They offered to take me, but I didn't want to leave California. I kept living in the same house and finished high school. Dad had a small life insurance policy. I waited tables at the local diner. Between the two, I had enough money to get by."

She sucked the inside of her cheeks, surprised the familiar pain when she talked about her parents wasn't as unbearable as it had been in years past. "I, um, got a scholarship to college. Finished in three years with a degree in civil engineering." She snorted. "It took me another year to land a job. Guess I should've picked a more feminine field like teaching or nursing.

"Anyway, that's about it. I still live in my parents' house. Don't date much." Alice glanced at her body. "I think I scare men away. I'm an engineer who likes mountain climbing. That usually describes men. Plus, I'm ungodly tall." She shrugged.

"Thank you for trusting me."

Was that what I was doing?

She smiled shyly. "You're welcome."

"You asked how I knew what Brent was." Jed took a deep breath. His forehead furrowed as if he were in pain. "It's because I'm a shifter. My other form is a wolf." He released her hand, watching her intently. Flecks of gold dusted his blue irises, lending his eyes an ethereal aspect.

Alice's heart thudded dully. She tried to feel frightened, but the most she could gin up was a crippling sadness. She'd started to care about Jed, but under the circumstances... Alice pushed her chair back. She didn't know much about shifters other than they were bad people who stole children and ate them—

Jed banged his fist down on the table, making the dishes rattle. "We do no such thing," he growled.

"Of course you'd say that." She got to her feet. "You said I could leave. I'll just collect my rucksack and—"

"Five more minutes and you can make that decision." He shut his eyes. When he opened them, his gaze zeroed in on her face. "Would you sit back down, or shall I stand?"

"Maybe you should stand." Her voice shook. She backed away.

He got to his feet. "I can't use magic to calm you like I did last night. If you decide to stay with me, it must be of your own free will. I've been alone for centuries—"

"H-how old are you?"

"Eight hundred sixty-seven years."

The breath whooshed out of her. Alice grabbed the back of the chair for support. Her eyes widened. Her breath came fast. She was in the presence of a living, breathing legend. A magical creature who'd been alive during the Crusades. "Jesus," she gasped. The implications were staggering. "How long will you live?"

A corner of his mouth twisted wryly. "Not forever, but a long time. We used to be free to roam and shift. Not for a long time. Our numbers are dwindling. Once human women vied with one another for the privilege of making love with us. It gave them status and power. Not anymore. Now we're shunned. Worse, we have to run free in our animal forms to spur the mating urge. Since most of us spend nearly all our time in our human skins, we're dying out."

He paused to suck in a breath, then hurried on. "I'm in these mountains because our four clans held a gathering to strategize—"

"Are all of you wolves?"

"No. The four clans are bears, mountain lions, wolves, and coyotes. There are bird clans too, but they're separate from us." A corner of his mouth twisted wryly. "If you keep interrupting me, I'll need more than five minutes."

Something softened inside her, maybe her compassion for underdogs. "Take all the time you need," she murmured. "I won't leave until you tell me you're done."

"I'm hoping you won't leave at all."

"I have to. My life—"

He shook his head. "Let me finish. I didn't mean never leaving this cabin. I meant never leaving me. I've told you about the gathering. I spent a day in my other form. When we headed down the mountain, we smelled your friend." Jed hesitated. "I'm certain he smelled us too. That's how they track us."

"Are you sure you didn't murder him?" She set her lips in a straight line. "After all, if he'd kill you—"

Jed closed the distance between them. He reached a finger and tilted her chin so she had to meet his gaze. "My lieutenants wanted to kill him. I admit, so did I, but we didn't."

"Why not?"

"All it would've done was bring the authorities here in droves." He shook his head, nostrils flaring. "No, it was better to get him as far from us as we could."

"Okay, what does this have to do with me?"

"I'm getting to that. I have access to my wolf senses when I'm human. They're not quite as strong, but they're much more acute than human perceptions. I smelled you as you descended the mountain. Your scent activated my mating urge."

He settled his hands on her shoulders. The energy from his body made her belly flutter oddly. Her nipples hardened into peaks. She sucked in a nervous breath.

"I knew you were the woman for me practically before I laid eyes on you."

"How?"

His ocean-blue eyes bored into her. "You've thought it odd you're so attracted to me. Don't bother denying it. I've seen it in your mind."

"So?" Alice felt oddly defensive, but it didn't put a dent in her arousal. "I-it's just because I've never—"

He laid a finger over her lips. "It's because of the shifter mate bond."

She wrenched away from him. Her breath came in little panting gasps. Confusion, fear, and lust lent a fine edge to her hyped-up emotions. "What's that?"

He licked his lips, and Alice realized he was almost as anxious as her. "It's an almost irresistible urge to merge our lives—body and soul—forever."

Her mind reeled. Questions buffeted her from all sides, but she didn't know what to ask first. "This mate bond thing, does it happen often?"

He shook his head and smiled sadly. "Unfortunately, it's quite rare and very special. It will open us to one another in a way few ever experience."

Breath whistled out of her. Alice felt frozen in place. Things like this only happened in stories, never to real people.

He cocked his head to one side. "No more questions? You're looking a little shell-shocked, sweetheart, which isn't surprising. Let me help. There are things you have to know before you make love with me."

Her mouth was dry. The few inches separating their bodies crackled with tension. "Not that I'm planning to make love with you, but what are they?" She tried to take a step back. He dropped his hands onto her shoulders again and held her in place.

"Shifter magic comes through semen. Your lifespan will increase. You will become more sensitive to what's in other people's minds. Your body will become stronger." He took a breath. "And the mate bond will link us. I feel it more intensely than you now, but that will change once I've shared your body."

Alice tried to wriggle free. Emotions buffeted her from all sides like a meteor storm gone awry.

"There's one more thing."

"Isn't what you've told me enough?"

"Like I said, one more thing. Once we've made love, you won't be able to get me out of your mind. The desire you feel now will pale in comparison to what you'll feel once we've mated. The same is true for me."

Alice ducked from beneath his hands. "I have to think, and I can't do that when you're so close." She glanced at him. His brows were drawn together. His red-gold hair shimmered, framing his handsome face. Longing shone from his eyes, but he gave her space.

"Surely you have questions," he prodded. "I'm probably damn near as nervous as you. I'm sure I've skipped over some important parts."

Alice was almost as aroused as she'd been the previous night. It was all she could do not to rub her thighs together. Her swollen labia pressed against the crotch of her trousers and her panties were drenched.

What am I thinking? I need to tell him thank you very much, I'll keep your secret, and now I'm leaving.

She opened her mouth, but what came out was, "What happens after we make love?" Alice shook her head. "Uh, what I meant to say was if we make love, what comes next."

"It's considerably more than just making love. Shifter love bonds are permanent. Once I take you, you'll be mine forever."

"Mine as in married?" Her voice squeaked. She coughed and took another slug of coffee. "Crap. I'm forgetting every manner I ever knew."

His eyes glowed tenderly. "Yes, mine as in married. You can keep as much or as little as you want of your current life. I have no objection to you working—"

"I certainly hope not." She settled her hands on her hips. "After all, it's 1936. Women do hold jobs."

"Does this mean—" It was his turn to look flustered. The incredible planes of his face radiated hope and love. "—you're actually considering my offer?"

"Well." Alice ignored the inner voice screaming at her to leave now while she still could. "I'm not getting any younger. No one's ever asked me to marry them before. I've never been with a man, and I like the idea of living longer and being even stronger than I am. Those are all plusses."

"There are cons."

She nodded. "Would I be Hunted right along with you?"

"I don't think so, but there aren't any guarantees. So far they haven't targeted our mates. Only us and our male children."

"Why the males?"

"They grow up to be shifters. Female children will share your magic."

"Can I have a few minutes to think about all this?"

"Yes, but you can't leave without making a decision. If you walk away from me, I will do something so you have no memory of me. It's safer for both of us that way."

Alice paced from one end of the cabin to the other. Her head was full; so was her heart. To finally find a man who wanted her... And what an incredible man. She felt his heat all the way across the cabin.

I want him. More than I think I've ever wanted anything.

Never mind that. Once I do this, it's permanent. Surely there are things I need to know before I leap into the unknown.

She took a steadying breath, and then another. "Where would we live?"

"Wherever you want. I really do hold a day job with Paramount, but I don't need to work. When you live as long as I have, money's not a problem."

Her eyes flooded with sudden tears. Alice wiped them away. She walked to him. "Would you come mountain climbing with me?"

Jed threw back his head and laughed. "If that's what makes you happy, of course. So long as you didn't mind if I was a wolf from time to time."

Leave, leave, leave, her inner maven shrieked.

Oh shut up.

"I've always done the right thing all my life and made responsible decisions, so this is hard for me—"

"Please, Alice. I'm sorry, I know I interrupted, but I'll love you and take care of you. You'll never want for anything, ever."

"How could you love me already?"

He grinned. "With the mate bond, it would be impossible for me not to love you, sweetheart. Shifters are special to Gaia, goddess of the Earth. She takes care of her own. The mate bond was her gift to us to ensure we were always happy and would never die out. Even though it hasn't worked quite as the goddess intended in modern time."

Her heart, a carefully tended wasteland, broke wide open.

She shoved aside not knowing him very well, certainly not well enough to love.

Maybe for once, I'll just trust the process and not analyze it to death.

She smiled at him. "It feels sort of like stepping off the edge of the world, but I accept."

CHAPTER 5

"Ou what?" Jed was stunned. He'd been certain she'd tell him thanks, but no thanks, and walk out the cabin door. Relief, gratitude, and love vied for ascendency. As if to say it could do them one better by adding lust to the equation, his cock sprang to attention.

"I said, I accept." She grinned back at him. "I'm an engineer, sweetie. We weigh the alternatives and make our choices. You just made me the best offer I've had in a long time. Now could we work on ridding me of my virginity?"

"I think that could be arranged."

He opened his arms. She nestled close, all warmth and curves. He toyed with telling her about Bron and Terin, but decided it could wait until he'd kicked her sensual side wide open. It wasn't as if she had to accept all three of them right away. They all lived so long, the process could unfold in its own time. Besides the mate bond would take care of any lingering doubts she might have and join her to his lieutenants, just as it did to him.

He hoped.

She tightened her arms around his back, splaying her hands across his shoulder blades. Jed felt her nipples harden where they pushed against his chest. Hungry for all of her, he bent his head and covered her mouth with his own. He nipped her lower lip, and she opened her mouth under his. When he sank his tongue inside, she sucked hungrily. Straddling his leg, she pressed herself against him.

He broke their kiss and smoothed strands of midnight dark hair away from her face. Her face was flushed, her lips parted. He smelled her lust, and it made him so hot it was all he could do not to rip her clothes off, bend her over the sofa, and plumb her from behind.

Plenty of time for that. I need to woo her, make her crazy with wanting me so it won't hurt as much when I rupture her maidenhead.

Jed took her hand and tugged gently. "Back to bed, sweetheart. I want to worship your body. It'll be easier if we're both comfortable."

She extricated her hand and walked ahead of him. When she got to the curtain, she shoved it aside and draped it over a hook. Next she tugged the drapes open as wide as they'd go. "That's better." She turned to him. "I've never seen a naked man before. I wanted enough light to appreciate you."

He quirked a brow. "Hope you're not disappointed. Now I'm truly fetching in my wolf form—"

She swatted his arm, and then glanced at her feet. "Need to get my shoes off. All you have on is slippers." Alice knelt and unlaced her stiff, mountaineering boots. He helped her upright, and she stepped out of them. Color stained her cheeks, and she sucked in an audible breath before reaching for the bottom edge of her top and yanking it over her head. Alice tossed her shoulders back and looked right at him. Her green eyes were defiant and burning with desire.

He gasped. Her breasts were amazing. Full, firm, and tipped with generous brown nipples. He reached toward one and circled it with a finger. Bending, he kissed it, flicking the sensitive tissue with his tongue while he suckled. It stiffened instantly. He sucked harder and was rewarded when she moaned and buried her hands in his hair.

Jed had planned to undress her slowly. It didn't seem either of them would have the patience. She straddled his leg again and rubbed herself against him. Her breath quickened. Reluctantly, he let go of her nipple and straightened.

"Don't stop," she panted.

"I'm not stopping, but we need to get rid of the rest of these clothes." He flicked at the bulge of his erection. "I'm not very comfortable, and I bet you're so wet your panties are sticking to you."

Alice giggled. She clapped a hand over her mouth. "I don't know what's gotten into me. For a minute there, I sounded a lot like a giddy schoolgirl."

She started on his buttons. In moments she pushed his shirt off his shoulders. "Oooh." She ran both hands down his chest. "Beautiful. Your skin is golden. Maybe it's the light, but you're glowing." She inclined her head and licked one of his nipples. "Are yours sensitive too?"

"Very." He placed a hand on either side of her head and tilted her face so he could kiss her. She threaded her arms around him, and the feel of her breasts against his bare chest was incredible. Her scent was heady, musk and honey mixed with pure sexual heat. He wanted to do everything all at once. Touch her, taste her, and fuck her.

Jed nuzzled her neck and laughed. "We're never going to get rid of our clothes." He reached for the fastenings of her climbing pants and undid them. She wriggled against his hands, and her pants slid to the floor. Next came her long underwear and panties.

"Not fair," she protested. "The best part of you is still covered." She fumbled with the buttons of his trousers. His cock sprang out. "Oh my." She took a breath and wrapped both hands around his shaft. "It's huge. I had no idea. Are all—?"

"Ssht." He laid a finger over her lips and stepped out of the tangle of pants puddled around his feet. His slippers snagged in them, but he left them where they lay. He tried to draw her into his arms, but she resisted.

"No. I want to look at you."

She walked behind him and ran her hands from his shoulders down over his buttocks. The muscles in his ass clenched. Curved against his stomach, his cock throbbed, heavy with need. Alice circled him and did the same exploration of the front of his body before settling her hands around his cock.

"Two can play that game."

He shoved a hand between her legs and rubbed her passion slick clit. She was just as ready as he was. Alice squirmed against his hand and made a small, moaning sound low in the back of her throat. He carefully pushed a finger deep inside her. Her muscles clenched around it. Hot as she was, he could make her come easily from just his fingers, but Jed had other ideas. He withdrew his hand and settled it in the curve of her waist.

"Legs don't want to stand anymore," she murmured and let go of his cock. Alice tugged the quilt out of the way. He marveled at the lush lines of her body. Her shoulders and thighs were shapely with muscle. A flat stomach flared to generous hips. Dark curls beckoned to him from between her legs.

Jed turned her to face him and wrapped his arms around her. Lost in the intoxicating scent of her arousal, he kissed her and let his hands roam down her back. They landed around the globes of her ass, and he pulled her close. He could've stood there kissing her forever, but his cock raged with lust.

He lifted his lips from hers. "Lie back, sweetheart." He maneuvered her onto the bed. Her hips moved of their own accord, thrusting upward.

"I know the first time hurts," she said. "It's all right."

She opened her arms, but he shook his head, got onto the bed next to her, and knelt over her body. Jed strung kisses down her neck to her breasts. He lingered over each, sucking and kissing her wonderful nipples before moving his head lower. He settled his mouth over the sensitive nub between her legs, pleased when she cried out at the intensity of the sensation. While he tongued her clit, he worked fingers deep inside, loosening her.

Her hips bucked against his face, clearly moving of their own accord. Little panting cries filled the air. She buried her hands in his hair and ground her body against him. Her pussy spasmed around his fingers, and he knew she was coming. He waited until her body settled, then slid up and positioned the head of his cock right at her opening. He rocked his pubic bone against her sensitive center, delighted when she pressed back hard. Slowly, ever so slowly, he sank his full length inside her, pushing past her barrier as gently as he could.

Jed supported his body on his arms so he could watch her face. "There," he said. "I'm inside. I won't move for a little. Just get used to how I feel."

Her muscles fluttered around him. She made small, experimental movements with her hips. Her delightful, full lips parted in a sensual smile. "It's fine. Just a little bit of discomfort, but it's gone now."

He smiled back, but didn't move. She rotated her hips. He kept his quiet. She moved her hands to his flanks and tugged.

"Tell me what you want," he said.

"I want you to move." Her voice was husky with passion.

He'd banked that one climax would whet her appetite for more. The mate bond would make her close to insatiable—at least in the beginning. "Like this?" He withdrew until just the tip of him teased her opening and moved it in a circular pattern. The restraint was killing him, but it was for a good cause. Once he settled into a rhythm, he'd come and come hard.

Her back arched. She threw her head back and gripped his hips. "Move goddammit. How can I figure this out if you don't do your part?"

Jed laughed. "As milady wishes." He pushed into her, but slowly, then pulled slowly back out. After a dozen strokes, his control crumpled. He drove himself into her hard and fast.

Alice groaned. She locked her legs around his hips and dug her nails into his sides.

Jed rode a ragged edge of control. He would make her come again before he did, no matter what it took. Her torso grew rosy, and her nipples hardened into points. With an instinctual knowledge, she held him inside her and ground her clit against the base of him. Her body spasmed around him while she shrieked her delight.

The next stroke took him over the edge. He juddered hard inside her so many times he wondered if he'd accidentally discovered a woman's secret about multiple orgasms. Breath rattled in his throat. His heart thudded against his ribs. Jed folded his arms, and his body collapsed atop hers.

The deed was done. She was his. Deep inside, his wolf howled its delight.

Bron and Terin. I have to tell her. Guilt pricked, cutting deep.

Soon. There's plenty of time before they get back.

~

ALICE WRIGGLED BENEATH HIS WEIGHT. Now that her brain wasn't fuzzy with lust, it worked overtime. His cock was still buried deep in her body. She flexed her muscles around him and was rewarded by a shower of sparks that ignited her nerve endings. She could come again. It was different with him inside than with her fingers, and oh so much more intense.

"Do you want more?" His voice was muffled in her hair.

"Yes, but we need to talk. We should have used a condom. What if—"

"I decide when my seed creates new life. Shifters are immune from human disease. You were a virgin. It's been long years since I had sex with anyone. I'd say you're quite safe on all fronts." He pulled out of her and rolled onto his side. Jed propped his head on his hand and gazed at her, his blue eyes brimming with tenderness.

Her body felt empty, bereft, without him inside. Alice turned her thoughts inward and took stock. "I feel...different." She sat up, crossed her legs Indian style, and looked at him.

"Yes. You would."

"It's more than not being a virgin anymore. There's something here." She tapped her breastbone. "It's like you've taken up residence inside me."

He nodded. "It's the mate bond. I feel it too. It will only grow and strengthen with time."

"It's, um, none of my business, but you said it had been a long time since you'd had sex. Have you had other mates?"

Jed shook his head. "No. It's not that I can't be sexual outside the mate bond, but mostly I haven't been interested. The bond enriches everything. I've lived such a long time, casual sex lost its appeal. It felt meaningless." He gave a short bark of a laugh. "My hand was a whole lot easier and more reliable when my balls ached because it was so long since they'd come."

"I want to understand more about the mate bond. Is there only one woman—?"

"No, it's not like that. Thank Christ." He rolled his eyes. "If it were, shifters would've died out eons ago. But there aren't many who ignite the bond. There has to be an intense attraction that runs deeper than the physical." He turned his amazing blue gaze right on her. "You, my dear, have a beautiful soul. I knew it before I ever saw you."

Her eyes widened. "Just from, um, smelling me come down the mountain?"

His mouth split in a broad grin. "That and strong instincts. It's one sideline benefit of being a shifter. I see things more clearly because of my lupine intuition."

"So there's more than a single possibility in terms of finding a woman to mate-bond with, but good candidates are rare."

"That's a decent summation, yes. They've gotten even rarer since humans have developed such an intense fear of us."

"Why is that?"

"Because we spend so little time in our animal form, it weakens our ability to sense a potential mate; it also dilutes our attractiveness to them."

She narrowed her eyes, thinking. Sadness washed through her. She pushed it aside. "I'm glad you weren't already taken."

He placed a hand on her thigh. "How could I have been? It sounds sappy, but I was waiting for you."

A thought came to her. She wanted to ask, but felt suddenly shy.

"You want to see what the animal half of our partnership looks like?"

Her cheeks grew warm. "I'd forgotten you can see into my head. Yes, maybe we could go outside and—"

"No." The vehemence of his tone startled her. "Too dangerous. I'll shift for you, but I'll do it in here."

"Will we still be able to talk?"

"Yes, but you'll hear my voice inside your head."

"I'd like it if you'd show me." Alice bit her lip. She didn't understand why it was so important for her to know his wolf side, but it was.

Jed got to his feet. His body was magnificent. Broad, well-muscled shoulders, slender hips and a wonderful ass. The slightest sprinkling of red-gold hairs circled his nipples. His cock was still half hard. Lust speared her. She wanted him again, but she ignored it.

The air took on a shimmery hue, bright and multitoned. In seconds, a black and silver timber wolf stood where Jed had been. The same blue eyes gleamed at her. Alice jumped off the bed and buried her hands in his thick coat. "You're beautiful this way too."

He turned his head and licked her bare leg. A delicious shiver ran up her spine. *"Why thank you."* His wolf voice was deeper than his human one, but with the same inflections.

Alice hunkered next to Jed and petted him shamelessly. To her surprise, tears welled. The affection she felt for him in all his forms was almost too much to take in. It filled her to the brim and spilled over in her tears.

"I could let you do that all day, but it's dangerous for me to stay this way." Jed stepped away from her. The air glowed. When it settled, his human self smiled at her.

"It won't be very comfortable, but I'm going to rinse myself off in the creek. Want to come?" She smiled back. "It's bad enough that my clothes stink."

"Sure, we can clean up. I'll even gin up a bit of magic so the water won't be quite as cold."

"You can do that?"

"You'll be able to also, once I teach you."

Warmth began in her midsection and spread through her body. "I feel like I've embarked on a grand adventure."

"You have." He dragged two robes off hooks and tossed one at her. "Here. It can double as a towel."

They went into the front room, and Jed pushed the cabin door open.

"But it was locked," she protested, walking through into pale, spring sunlight.

"Not for very long. I unlocked it once you went to bed."

"Humph. You might've told me."

"I couldn't chance having you leave before I'd made my pitch. I was willing to risk you being angry with me." He took her hand and led her along a cleared path. "Easier on your feet over here."

"No more secrets."

"No more secrets," Jed agreed. "It's part of the mate bond." An odd look crossed his face, but before she could delve into what it meant, he pointed toward the creek. "A waist deep pool is just past that boulder. It's where we rinse off. The water's more contained and easier to warm."

He draped his robe over a flat rock and reached for hers. Alice grinned and handed it to him. Maybe she'd only imagined the odd look. "You just want to see me naked."

"You bet!" Jed slipped into the water. He shut his eyes and waved his hands in an intricate pattern in front of him. "Come on." He crooked a finger at her. "Not bath temperature by any means, but better than the rest of the creek."

She dipped her foot in. "Gee, it's actually tepid. How'd you do that?"

"I drew heat from the earth's crust. Wolf shifters have an affinity for earth magic. The other clans each have their own special element."

She got into the water and sat on the sandy creek bottom, letting the stream flow over her. Part of her hair was still in its sloppy braid. The rest hung free. She untangled its strands and tilted her head back to wash the sweat out of it. "There's a lot for me to learn. Is any of this written down anywhere?"

"Once upon a time, yes. Not anymore. We've been Hunted mercilessly for several hundred years."

"You'll teach me?"

He nodded. "Of course. We need to talk about what happens next."

"When do you suppose your friends will be back? I suppose they're shifters too?"

"They ought to show up in the next couple of hours. And yes, they're wolf shifters. Terin and Bron are my lieutenants. Together, we manage the wolf clan and make a family unit."

"How many are in the clan?"

"Just shy of a thousand in this country. Double that if you count the rest of the world."

Alice tried to latch onto her usually sharp analytic skills. There was so much she didn't know, it was tough to decide where to begin asking questions. "Do you travel to, uh, oversee things?"

"Yes, more in astral form than the way you're thinking about it, though."

"This just gets deeper and deeper, doesn't it?"

He took her hand under the water. "It will feel pretty overwhelming at first. I'll do everything I can to help you. When are you expected back?"

"No one's expecting me anywhere until the end of this week. I took a few vacation days from work."

He knitted his brows in thought. "One of us will go down the trail with you and see you safely to your car. You'll drive to the hospital to check on Brent because you ran into some strangers who told you he'd been hurt. Brent will be suspicious. Do what you can to set his mind at ease. Then return to your house and job. I'll find you and we'll go through the *pretend we just met* ritual in case anyone's paying attention—"

"It will be a whirlwind courtship since I want you where I can lay eyes and hands on you," she interrupted. Alice couldn't stop smiling. Tingly warmth that had nothing to do with the water swooshed through her. "I don't know when I've felt this happy. Certainly not since Mom and Dad died."

He bent his head toward her and kissed her forehead. "That's exactly how I want you to feel, sweetheart. Happy and fulfilled."

They lolled in the water until Jed said they needed to get moving so they'd be dressed when Bron and Terin showed up. Alice snuggled into his arms. "I hate to get up. Being here with you feels so right."

"That's because it is." He tightened his hold on her.

A savage whoop sent her heart spinning into overdrive. Alice tore herself away from Jed's embrace and gazed wildly about. "What was that?"

"Damn! I knew we should've gotten out of the water sooner. It's just my boys."

"Wahoo!" Red hair streaming around him, Terin cannonballed into the water. He'd shucked his clothes somewhere between the cabin and the creek.

"Double wahoo. You got us a woman. Our new mate. I smell the bond. Nice work, boss." Bron splashed into the creek and sat down in the water. He grinned at Alice. "Welcome to the pack, sister."

"From me too," Terin said through a huge smile. "Sorry. I forgot my manners."

The happiness inside Alice winked out, replaced by bleak resignation. Something was desperately wrong and she had no idea what it was. Focusing on Jed, she gritted out, "What the hell are they talking about?"

CHAPTER 6

"Leave her be," Jed snapped at the men, ignoring her question.

"But you're mated. I can smell it, and I sense the bond," Terin protested. "That means—"

"Quiet. We hadn't gotten to that part yet."

"What part?" Alice would've drawn herself up to her full height if she weren't naked. She sank deeper in the water, tucked her knees in front of her breasts, and wound her arms around them.

She gazed at Terin. He was a very good-looking man. Just as handsome as Jed, but in a different style of masculine beauty. Her nipples pebbled beneath the water, and a corner of her mind recoiled in horror.

Am I going to turn into a wanton and want to fuck every shifter I see?

She shook her head hard. "I'm quite interested in whatever Jed didn't quite get around to telling me." Sarcasm dripped from her words, but she didn't try to modulate it.

Terin's amber eyes skittered away from hers. "Uh, it's not my place."

"Damn straight," Jed muttered. "How about if the two of you give us some privacy so the lady can get dressed?"

Bron rolled his dark eyes. "Aye-aye, oh fearless leader."

He got to his feet. His cock jutted in front of him, long, thick, and beautiful. Alice got an eyeful before he turned and plodded through the water to shore. It was all she could do to keep from launching herself out of the water after him. Terin followed. When he stood, his back was to her, but Alice had no doubt his member was just as hard as the other shifter's.

Scenes of her making love to all three of them flashed before her eyes. Alice got hold of herself. The thought was so absurd as to be laughable, no matter how aroused she was.

She rounded on Jed. "What the hell happened to *no secrets?*" Her voice was raised, angry, but she didn't waste energy toning it down. "It doesn't take a genius IQ to figure out you've signed me up for some sort of plural marriage hell."

"It's not like that." Anguish underscored his quiet words. "I was going to tell you right after we got out of the creek. Truly I was. If you focus your mind to see into mine, you'll see I'm telling you the truth. It's part of the magic that—"

"I don't care about your fucking magic. I don't want any part of it." Alice stormed out of the water, wringing water from her hair as she went. She grabbed her robe and shrugged into it.

"But we're mated—" He followed her out of the water, hands held before him in supplication. "The mate bond is a family bond. Terin and Bron and I are—"

"Undo it."

She glared through slitted eyes. "I thought you cared about me. Now it seems like you were hunting for a trollop to pass between all of you. Is it just you three, or is it any old wolf shifter who happens along? I heard they do that in Alaska with the Eskimos—the whole wife-swapping deal."

Alice pounded a fist into her thigh. What she wanted to do was shove it through Jed's face—right after she fucked him again. She told her pussy to leave her alone. Tears threatened to spill down her face. "I'm not interested. Not today. Not tomorrow. Never. You should've told me."

"Yes, I should have. And I was going to—"

"When?" She turned away. "Christ, I can't believe I'm still even talking with you. I need to get my clothes and get out of here. Do whatever you were going to do to wipe all of this out of my memory." To her horror, a sob followed her words, and then one more. Her throat thickened until it was hard to breathe.

Jed's hands landed on her shoulders. She spun away. "No! Don't touch me. Not anymore."

Alice took off running. Stones and branches cut into her feet, but she was beyond caring. Jed's footsteps crashed behind her. She ran faster. A shadow crossed the forest floor in front of her. Blinded by tears, it took her a moment to realize it was a mountain lion.

The creature sprang. Its weight drove her to the ground. Alice screamed. A rank smell made her gag. The cat bit into her shoulder, and shooting pain lanced through her. Alice grappled with the cat, trying to pry it off, but it raked sharp claws down her hands. A deep, throaty growl filled the air. Blood spilled down her arm, its hot, coppery odor mingled with the putrid smell of cat. Something else heavy landed atop her.

"You're free. Roll. Run for the cabin." Jed's voice sounded in her mind.

She rolled away from the wolf engaged in mortal combat with the mountain lion. Alice screamed for Bron and Terin. If

Jed got himself killed defending her, she'd never be able to live with herself.

"Run, goddammit. I've got things under control."

"Like hell you do." Alice stared at the enraged cat. It had traded her body for Jed's. Its teeth were buried in his neck. Blood darkened the wolf's fur. She picked up a good-sized rock, intent on bashing the cat in the head. Branches crackled. Two more wolves, one nearly black, the other more reddish, sprang on the cat. She stepped back so their tumbling bodies wouldn't knock her to the ground and gripped her rock. If things went to hell, she'd jump into the fray.

She swallowed, but her throat was so dry the tissue just grated against itself.

Jed. Oh, Jed.

In that moment, she knew the mate bond had worked its magic. In spite of her harsh words and bravado about leaving, she loved Jed. Adored him beyond hope and reason. Fondness for Bron and Terin had taken root inside her as well.

"No," she murmured. "I can't lose you—none of you. Not so soon."

Not ever, an inner voice corrected.

Terin and Bron had drawn the cat a short distance away. Jed's wolf form sprawled on the ground. He wasn't moving. She threw herself over his body. A high, keening cry filled the air. Alice barely recognized the agonized sound as hers. She moved her hands carefully over the wolf's body.

Where the hell did you find an animal's heartbeat?

Just when she was certain he was dead, faint movement beat beneath her fingertips. Relief so intense it was hard to bear spilled through her. She shoved the pain from her own injuries aside and pulled his body into her arms.

"You can't die," she whispered in his ear. "You're my mate. I

—I'm sorry for the things I said. I was upset. Angry. Not thinking straight—"

Arms lifted her from Jed's body. She tried to pull free. "No," she moaned. "He needs me. He has to know I'm sorry, that we'll work things out—"

Jed's two lieutenants held her firmly between them. "Ssht. I'm Terin," the redhead said. "The cat's dead. We've got to get Jed back to the cabin. We can work on healing him there."

"You're injured also. Follow us," Bron commanded. "We've got to do something about the cat. It'll attract every predator within five miles, but that will have to wait."

The two naked men suspended Jed's wolf form between them. They carried him almost reverently. Alice scrambled to her feet. Her shoulder burned and throbbed. Her robe was wet with blood. Momentarily dizzy, she clung to a tree trunk until her head cleared.

When she pushed through the cabin door, Jed lay on the floor still in wolf form. Dark head bent, Bron chanted over him. Alice started forward, but Terin grabbed her arm. He placed a finger over his lips then drew her toward the back of the cabin.

"Bron must concentrate," he whispered low in her ear. "Jed's barely clinging to life."

"There's a telephone in the lodge," she whispered back. "Maybe you could run down there, break in and call for—" She caught herself and shook her head. Of course they couldn't get a doctor to come. Not to treat a shifter.

"Don't give up hope," Terin murmured. "Jed is strong, and Bron is one of our most gifted healers. While he works, let me treat your wound." He pushed the robe off her shoulders. Alice made a grab for it. She was naked beneath its fabric. Terin batted her hand away. "Don't be foolish. Do you want an infection to set in?"

Alice gritted her teeth. No one had clothes on. She let her robe slide to the floor and gazed at Terin. Leaner than Jed, his hair was long enough to reach the middle of his back. The planes of his face were set in severe lines, but he was classically handsome with clean, even features. Her body yearned for the comfort of his arms. She chided herself for being a whore. Jed lay near death. It wasn't a time to think about sex.

"Are you strong enough to walk to the creek?" Terin was still whispering. "I'd like to scrub this. Once it's clean, I'll draw earth magic to see it heals. Lucky you haven't lost too much blood." He made a faint clucking sound. "The worst thing about puncture wounds is infection."

"There's a pump in here," she whispered back.

"Too noisy. Bron's still chanting. I feel his magic. Best for Jed if we don't disturb either of them."

Though she didn't want to leave Jed, Alice followed Terin back to the pool. At his direction, she sank her body into the water. He didn't offer to warm it. Goosebumps rose. She stayed submerged until her body ached from the cold and scrubbed the wound with sand like Terin instructed.

"All right. It's enough. You can come out." His voice was gruff.

Grateful there wasn't a breeze to chill her further, Alice made her way to where Terin stood on the bank. He inspected her shoulder with its semicircle of puncture wounds, then laid a hand over it. She started. Energy flowed from his body into hers. It was palpable, like an electric shock. He placed his other hand on her other shoulder and murmured in an incomprehensible language.

The sharp, throbbing pain receded. Terin removed his hands. He nodded, looking pleased with his work. "It's healed."

Alice couldn't see the wound, but she touched where it had been with probing fingers. Her eyes widened with surprise.

"My skin is whole." She took a step back and locked gazes with him. "How'd you do that?"

"I already told you. Earth magic. You're bonded to us, which is why it worked so well. You are of the earth, just as we are." He looked away from her. "I owe you an apology. Bron and I shouldn't have mobbed you like we did. We talked about it before the cat attacked and realized Jed hadn't really had enough time to do much more than mate with you."

"It's all right. I was a royal bitch." She bit her lip. "Jed. If he dies because he was defending me—"

"He can't," Terin cut in, his amber eyes fierce. "We need him. He's our alpha. There isn't another who can take his place as clan leader."

Alice turned her energies inward. "I feel...something. It's like a slender, glowing cord that links me to him." She closed her teeth over her lower lip. "And to you and Bron as well, but those threads aren't as thick."

Terin nodded. "It's the mate bond. We are pack. You're part of us now. You'll come to understand the symbols better as you live with them." He shut his eyes just before his forehead creased.

"Damn it." He spun and raced for the house.

"What? What's happened?" Fear turned her guts to water. Alice sprinted after him. By the time she rushed through the open cabin door, Terin had joined Bron on the floor next to Jed's wolf form. Both shifters had their hands buried in Jed's lush pelt. They chanted frantically in the language Terin had used to patch her shoulder.

The wolf's labored breathing caught and slowed.

"No!" She raced to Jed's side and fell to her knees, then to her belly. She took his head between her hands and spoke softly into his ear. "I don't know if you can hear me, beloved, but don't leave me. Please, please don't leave me. I'm so sorry about the things I said. I love you. I want us to have a life together."

Her words ran into one another. Time dribbled past. Tears dripped off her nose and fell into Jed's fur. She prayed to any deity who would listen to save her love. The wolf's body shimmered and took on an unearthly glow. For one horrible moment, she was certain Jed had died, but then her fingers touched warm, living flesh.

Terin's hands settled over hers. He blew out a relieved-sounding breath. "Jed is a bit stronger. At least he was able to shift. Bron will be exhausted once this is done. Come off to the side and let him finish."

Alice staggered to her feet and fell into a nearby chair. Terin eyed her. "Thank you. I believe you reached Jed, and it helped call him back. We're a family. That means we do whatever it takes to ensure our survival."

"I don't know if you can explain it to me, but what's Bron doing to save Jed?"

Terin knit his auburn brows together. "He's pouring his own life essence into him, mixing it with earth magic, and mending the broken places in Jed's body. The first task was to stabilize him enough to get him back to human form."

"Jed said the mate bond would give me some magic." She hesitated. "Is what you're doing, where you manipulate earth magic, something I could learn?"

"Yes. It will take time, though, and it's anyone's guess how strong the power will run in you."

Terin pulled a chair next to hers and took her hands. "First, I need to explain a little to you. Some of it you've guessed, but hearing it may help. Your primary mate bond is with Jed. He will be your mated one—er, husband—in the eyes of the world."

Terin took a measured breath. "We three are a pack. As Jed's mate, we welcome you." A lopsided grin lit the sharp planes of his face and made his amber eyes glow. "Part of that welcome is physical. We, that is Bron and I, want to be a part of your lovemaking with Jed. It's what packs do. The alpha mates and we all share." Terin hesitated, but his gaze bored into hers. "We would always care for you and respect you, just as he does."

"I—"

"Uh-uh." Terin let go of her hands. "Just think about it. No need to give any of us an answer right now. We live for a long time. We can wait for you while the mate bond takes root and grows."

She smiled crookedly. "You may not have to wait very long. This mate bond thing, it tugs at me like—"

Jed coughed.

Alice leapt from her chair and bounded to his side. His coppery skin was pale. Bron helped him sit with his back propped against the sofa and his legs splayed on the hooked rag rug in front of the fireplace. Looking nearly as pallid as Jed, he staggered to his feet and clumped to the kitchen. When he returned, he had a bottle of whiskey clutched in his hand. He took a swig and handed it to Jed who drank before passing it to Terin, who'd also huddled close.

"Thank Christ." Alice sank to the floor next to Jed. "I was so frightened I'd lost you." She reached a tentative hand and laid it on his thigh.

"You don't have to treat me as if I were made of glass." He draped an arm around her shoulder and pulled her close. "I'm healed. When it works, earth magic is quick. Bron did a good job. In an hour or so, I'll have my full strength back." He pried the whisky bottle out of his lieutenant's hand and took a nip then passed it to her.

Alice looked at it, shrugged, and slugged some back. "I don't usually drink before five. Hell, I don't usually drink at all."

"This is a special occasion," Terin said. "You lost a fair amount of blood from the cat bite. Nothing like good Irish whiskey to spur your body to make more."

With a resurgence of his understated humor, Jed chuckled. "None of us needs an excuse to drink. What a hell of a morning. I was scared out of my wits when that wretched cat came out of nowhere and attacked. They're supposed to sleep during the day—"

"It was a mother with early season kits," Terin broke in. "She was hungry. Game's not all that plentiful yet."

Bron dragged a hand down his face, distorting his features. "We tried to give her a chance to live, but she was beyond reasoning with. One of her litter had already died. To her, we were a hedge to ensure the rest survived."

"You, uh, spoke with her." Alice ran up hard against the way things were supposed to be in the world.

"Of course." Bron sounded offended. "We never take life without giving our victim a choice."

"Well, almost never." Terin grunted. "With Hunters all bets are off."

"What will happen to the other kits?" Alice asked, feeling sorry for the motherless creatures.

Bron shook his head. "They'll die without their mother, but there's nothing we can do about that. Another mountain cat would kill them. We tried to locate a shifter who might care for them, but no one answered our call."

Alice got to her feet. "Keep talking. I'm going to collect my clothes from where I left them on the bed. It's too cold in here to be naked."

Jed exchanged glances with his lieutenants. "If the two of

you could clear out of here, it would give me a chance to talk with Alice about—"

"I already did," Terin said.

Alice came back into the front room and sat next to Jed. Her clothes were so dirty, she hated to put them back on, but there wasn't any help for it.

Jed looked at her appraisingly and blew out a considered breath. An expression that might've been hope flitted across his face. "Terin spoke to you about the mate bond, eh? I'd have thought you'd run screaming down the mountainside, but I'm really glad you didn't. Would you like some privacy so we can talk?"

Her lips parted. She bit the lower one. "I don't think so. The way Terin explained it, we're all part of a family. If there's talking to be done, doesn't that mean we do it together?"

Jed smiled. It was a pale ghost of his previous grins, but happiness glowed in the depths of his eyes. "What happened to being so angry you wanted to scratch my eyes out?"

She shrugged. "We don't really know one another all that well yet. I have a temper. I suppose it comes from the McNeil side of the family. Like all Irish, my anger flares, burns hot, and goes out. Usually pretty damned fast. Dad was the same way, though, and he was a Carey and more British than Irish. His bark was always worse than his bite." A familiar sadness tugged at her. "Dad would've liked you."

Jed inclined his head. "Really. He would have approved of you marrying a shifter?"

Alice laughed. "I don't see why not. He held conversations with spirits and Sidhe and all manner of Irish ghosts. I always believed it was why Mom married him. Made her feel like she was back in the Old Country."

Bron nodded tiredly. "It's why she's our mated one. She

already had magic from her Irish ancestors. I'm going to curl up in a corner and fall on my face for an hour or so."

"Thank Christ, you're in better shape than I thought you'd be," Terin muttered.

"What a good idea," Jed concurred. "Could you use a spot of rest, sweetheart?"

"Sure. Then I probably need to head out after Brent. It's possible he'll tell the authorities to send someone to look for me."

"Mmph," Jed muttered. "Hadn't thought of that."

"I think we're safe until tomorrow," Terin said. "The Hunter was still out cold when we dropped him at the hospital. After the doctor thanked us, he said something about a coma."

Jed's gaze zeroed in on Bron. "What did you do?"

Bron's angular face softened as he smiled. "You know me too well. I simply made certain it would be a while before he woke up. Wanted to have plenty of time to get back here and clear out in case he made shifter noises and people came sniffing after us."

"I'm going outside to see to the cat's carcass," Terin said. "Then I'll get some rest too." He turned and strode out the door, latching it behind him.

Using the sofa as a crutch, Jed levered himself to his feet and held his hands out to Alice. She grasped them and stood. "Maybe an hour's nap would help." She glanced out a window. "With all that's happened, it's hard to believe, but I don't think it's much past noon."

"Doesn't matter what time it is," Jed murmured, "we all need sleep. You'll find you don't require as much as you used to, but an hour's downtime will do wonders for all of us."

CHAPTER 7

Alice woke to the pressure of Jed's arm around her waist and the jut of his erect cock against her backside. His breath was warm against her hair. Careful not to disturb him, she slithered from under his arm. She needed to pee. The small hitch in Jed's breathing told her he was still asleep. Good. He'd nearly died. No matter what he said, he needed all the rest he could get.

She gazed at his face. The bone structure was so beautiful, it could've been sculpted by one of the ancients. High cheekbones blended into a strong jaw. Beneath full, sensual lips, a cleft set off his chin. Deep in her soul, she knew she'd never tire of looking at him. His eyes fluttered open. Alice bent and kissed his cheek.

"Sleep, love. I'll be right back."

He murmured something and rolled over.

Alice walked out of the bedroom, her bare feet quiet. She held the curtain so it wouldn't rustle. Terin was stretched out on the sofa. Bron sat at the kitchen table. He quirked a questioning brow. She held up a finger to tell him she'd be right back and slipped out the cabin's door. On her way back from the outhouse, she glanced at the angle of the sun. Maybe three o'clock.

Bron had moved to one of the wooden chairs on the front porch. He patted the one next to it. "Terin got a chance to talk with you, but I didn't."

Alice sat. Most of her sore muscles were better, probably a byproduct of Terin's intervention. She gazed into Bron's bottomless, dark eyes. Something clicked within her, and his dusky beauty sang to her. An image of his erection as he'd left the creek burned across her eyes. Lust pierced her. She shook her head.

How can I want all of them? It seems wrong somehow.

No, a different inner voice spoke up, *it's the rightest thing I've ever found.*

Her lips curved into a smile. "Thank you for saving Jed."

"I love him. He's like a father and brother to me. Aside from that, we need him. The war with humans is heating up. Jed is wiser than the other clan leaders, more subtle. I fear the others will lead their shifter packs to their doom."

"How?"

"By engaging humans in direct combat. We got permission at the gathering to kill not just Hunters, but other humans as well. At first Terin and I were caught up in the bloodlust, but Jed brought us to our senses."

"I have a lot to learn. I'm hoping the three of you will teach me. I'm sorry I was such a highhanded witch when we first met."

A corner of Bron's mouth turned up, forming a boyish grin. "No apologies needed." Color stained his tanned cheeks, turning them a deeper copper. "I'm hoping you'll come to see Terin and me in a more, um, acceptable light. You're Jed's chosen one. We'll love and care for you too, if you'll let us."

Alice nodded. "I think I'm beginning to understand. It's not what I thought at first. We're like a wolf pack—"

"And why wouldn't we be?" Jed's half-laughing voice came from the open cabin door. "It's what we are: wolves."

"I wish I could be one." Alice clapped a hand over her mouth. Her face warmed. "Where the hell did that come from?"

"From the place deep inside you where the mate bond is anchored," Bron answered.

Jed stepped onto the porch. "Terin's still asleep. I don't want to wake him." He covered the small space to Alice and drew her out of the chair and into his arms. She turned her face up and he kissed her.

She wound her arms around his body and opened her mouth under his. The spicy, exotic scent that was his and his alone filled her nostrils. Sexual heat roared through her, setting her nerves ablaze. Her nipples hardened where they pushed against his chest. Her pussy turned to molten liquid. Jed's erection pressed against her stomach. Alice thrust against it. She couldn't wait to feel him inside her body again.

Bron.

Alice jerked away from Jed's body. She'd been so lost in lust, she'd forgotten the other shifter. He stared at the two of them, naked hunger burning in the depths of his eyes. The front of his trousers belled out from his erection. Suddenly shy, Alice wanted him too. She turned to Jed.

His lips curved in a knowing smile. "He'd like to join us, but it's up to you, Alice."

"Yes." Bron licked his lips. "It's up to you. I can go out back and take care of myself."

Confusion mingled with lust. Now that she knew him a little, she liked Bron, respected him. He'd saved Jed's life, risking his own in the process. He and Terin had sprung into action to save her from the mountain cat.

"You'll have to teach me." She looked from one to the other. "But God help me if I don't want both of you."

Jed's face split into a merry grin. "Come on. We'll lay some blankets out behind the cabin."

He gripped one of her hands. Bron took the other. Their bodies jockeyed against one another as all three of them tried to fit down the steps. Alice giggled, but quietly. She didn't want to disturb Terin.

Past the stair gauntlet, Bron tapped Jed's arm. "How about if you do the blankets? I haven't so much as kissed Alice yet."

Jed's blue eyes glittered mischievously. "Sure. See you two momentarily."

Bron closed his arms around her from behind. He strung kisses down her neck and pressed his erection into her butt. His breath burned where it trailed down her bare skin. Alice twisted in his arms. He held her against him so hard she felt his heartbeat where her face pressed into the hollow of his shoulder.

"I won't last long," he murmured. "Haven't been inside a woman for a long time."

She snorted. "Up until this morning, I was a virgin. I'm so inexperienced, I won't even notice." She slipped a hand between them and curved it around his erection. He groaned and thrust against her. "Come on." She grinned at him. "I feel like a kid who just discovered the very best candy store in the world. I want to see what this—" she squeezed his cock "— looks like for more than those few seconds when you jumped out of the creek."

"First, let me taste you." He held onto her and bent his head to kiss her. His lips covered hers. He kissed differently than Jed, more tentative at first. She opened her mouth to him, and he sank his tongue inside it. He tasted of heat and promise, of forests and feral desire. His tongue sparred with hers, and he tightened his hands on her ass. His cock jumped against her belly. He groaned around their kiss. She pressed her body into his. Desire arced from the top of her head all the way to her toes.

She broke away from the kiss before he brought her to orgasm from just rubbing against him. Alice grabbed his hand and hurried around the house. Jed was already naked, lying on the blankets, and stroking his hard on. Surprised at her lack of modesty, Alice drew her top over her head and undid the fastenings on her pants. Jed crooked a lazy finger at her. She sank to her knees next to him. Bron knelt on Jed's other side. Alice gazed at his body. He was built a lot like Jed with a lean, muscled form. His nipples were darker and his erection sprang from a mat of coal black hair. He glanced at Jed. Something passed between them. She felt the energy resonate through the mate bond.

"Come here, sweetheart, and straddle me." Jed pulled one of her legs over his body. She lowered herself onto his shaft. Lust rocketed through her. Her clit swelled. Her nipples grew so hard they ached. Jed settled his hands on her hips. Bron leaned toward her and took a nipple in his mouth. He suckled her and stroked her body while Jed's cock twitched deep inside. Bron switched to her other breast. He worked his erection with a hand. The hotter he got, the harder he sucked on her.

Alice rocked her clit against the base of Jed's erection. Her back arched. She reached for Bron's cock, displacing his hand. Uncertain at first, Alice stroked him. He covered her hand with his and showed her the rhythm he needed. Jed's blue eyes ignited with desire. He pressed his fingers between her legs and rubbed her sensitive nub. Bron groaned. His cock jumped in her hand, then jumped again. Hot semen splattered her. Jed rubbed her clit harder. She came, spasms shooting through her, while still clutching Bron's throbbing cock.

Still buried deep inside her body, Jed rolled her over. He drew himself out and then drove his cock home. Bron moved a hand between their bodies and tweaked her clit. He pulled and rubbed in a circular motion that damn near drove her crazy. Alice shrieked and moaned. Her pussy convulsed around Jed's cock as it juddered deep inside her. She clawed his back. She'd never been so high. She wanted to come again and again.

Jed bent and kissed her, then pulled out. "No, I don't want you to leave," she murmured.

"Fair is fair." Jed lay next to her and smoothed hair away from her face. "You want Bron too."

The minute he said it, she knew she did. Her gaze locked on the shifter's dark eyes. His cock was hard again, standing straight out in front of him. "Turn over, darling," he said. "Up on your hands and knees."

She flipped onto her belly and drew her limbs under her. The heat of Bron's body seared her as he moved his cockhead to her opening and swirled it in tiny circles. Jed reached beneath her and took a nipple in each hand. She arched her back and moved her hips suggestively, but Bron stayed where he was. He cupped her vulva and rubbed her clit. Her hips bucked.

"Now," she cried. "What are you waiting for?"

Bron laughed. The sound was exultant. "An invitation." He sank into her, gripping her hips. Jed moved so he could reach her clit. He rubbed her sensitive flesh while Bron plumbed her. Alice was beside herself. Her entire body was on fire. She hovered on the brink of coming until she couldn't stand it anymore and tumbled over the edge. Bron's cock jerked inside her. It heightened her climax to know he was coming right along with her.

The three of them collapsed into a satisfied heap, panting. Alice laughed. "I could get used to this."

"And it will just keep getting better," Jed said, grinning like a fool.

Bron nuzzled her neck. "Thank you," he whispered in her ear. "That was wonderful, amazing, stupendous—" His cock twitched inside her.

"Hey, looks like I slept through all the fun." Terin threw himself onto the blankets next to them. He made a grab for one of her breasts and twirled her stiff nipple. Sparks shot from it to her hypersensitive pussy. "How about it, Alice? I'm fresh. Let's give these two a chance to recover."

Three beautiful men. All for me.

A laugh bubbled from a reservoir of joy deep within her. "I'm starting to see some of the advantages here." She gazed at Terin's penis. It was as thick as Jed's, but a little shorter. His body had better defined muscles and his chest a bit more hair. Desire for him set her nerve endings thrumming.

"We've barely begun, darling." Bron pulled his still hard cock out of her. "I could stay there forever, but in the interest of fairness..."

Terin turned her onto her back and moved between her legs. His amber eyes glazed over with heat. He lowered his head and kissed her breasts, laving both of them while he sank a hand between her legs. Surprised by her boldness, but too randy to care, Alice made a grab for his cock. It jerked in her hands.

He repositioned himself so he could look at her. "You're catching on quick, Alice. Tell me what you want."

She opened her legs and drew him atop her. He groaned and buried himself inside. She gripped his hips and locked her legs around him. Her back bowed, and her head fell back. Jed bent forward and kissed her. He broke away from the kiss and positioned his body so his cock slipped into her mouth.

Alice gagged, but then she figured it out and used her hand to stroke his shaft and control how deep he went. She tasted herself on him, and it made her even hotter. The feel of his ridged flesh in her mouth was delicious. She played with his shaft, teasing it with fingers and tongue. Then she experimented with little nibbles, listening for changes in Jed's breathing to tell her what was most intense for him. She felt like a sex goddess with three men worshipping her. Having a cock in her mouth was almost more of a turn-on than having one in her pussy.

Terin plumbed her. Thrusting against him, she met him stroke for stroke as she sucked on Jed's cock. A now familiar tightening in her belly told her she was close to release.

"Yes, darling. Come with me," Terin urged.

Her muscles clenched and then she came, spasms surging through her. His cock swelled inside her and juddered hard. She would've held onto his hips, but her hands were busy with Jed.

Terin pulled out. She felt empty, gestured for him to come back. A cock slipped inside, but it felt different. Through the lust-haze she realized it was Bron. Someone's hands fondled her breasts. Jed thrust harder into her mouth. His hand worked his shaft atop hers. He pulled away. She watched him stroke his swollen member, watched semen arc out of it and spatter on the ground.

It made her so hot she thought she'd pass out from wanting sex, more sex, all the sex she could get. Her hands closed around Bron's hips. She urged him to fuck her faster. Terin twirled her nipples harder. Screaming her joy, her body convulsed around Bron's cock.

"Right behind you," he panted. His cock jerked inside her and jerked again.

"Holy Christ," Alice said when she could talk again. "If I'd known how much I liked this, I wouldn't have stayed a virgin all these years."

"We're glad you did," the three men said in unison just before all of them dissolved in laughter.

"Let's rinse off in the creek," Jed said. "Then we need to make plans and get out of here."

~

JED FOLLOWED Alice to the pool where they'd bathed earlier in the day. Dark hair cascaded down her back to her butt. Thick and curly, it swirled around her when she walked. She had the most incredible body. Limber and lithe. And an unconscious sexuality that made him hotter than hell. It had amped his pleasure tenfold to watch her with his pack mates. The sexual energy they made as a group was ever so much more intense than one on one couplings. He grinned.

Let's hear it for the mate bond.

She turned to him. "So can we always be like this? No one gets jealous, no one storms out. No one feels they're not getting enough."

He pulled her against him and kissed her deeply. Terin and Bron chugged by on their way to the water. They slugged him in the arm as they passed and gave him a thumbs up sign. Jed pulled away from Alice and laughed. "It's kind of like a big puppy pile. The mate bond ensures we always love and respect everyone in the pack."

"Will sex always be with all four of us?"

"You little vixen. I've created a monster. Your eyes are gleaming with lust. Would you like it to always be all of us?"

She cocked her head to one side, her eyes narrowed in thought. "I don't know. This is all so new to me. I liked it when it was just you and me, but I liked it with all of us too."

"It will be different things at different times. All of us work. We won't always all be in the same place when one of us wants sex." He shrugged. "Come on, let's rinse off. I know Bron thinks your buddy will be out for a while yet, but it would be much better for you to be waiting at the hospital when he wakes up than for him to start spewing shifter crap before you get there."

She slipped into the water. Jed followed. One of the others had warmed it.

"Thank you." Bron laid his hands on either side of her head and kissed her forehead.

"Yes, many thanks for accepting us." Terin kissed her too. "From the looks of things, I was sure I was destined to jack off for at least a couple of years while I listened to you and Jed fucking."

"Yeah, and he would've made me watch." Bron laughed.

"Watch, hell. I would have made you do me."

"In your dreams." Bron splashed water at him. "I love you, brother, but love only goes so far."

Jed laughed indulgently. He loved Bron and Terin. And now their pack was complete. Joy warmed him. It had been a long wait, but Alice was worth it. He stood and helped her out of the water.

Back in the cabin, Jed gathered her things. He strapped her axe to her pack and made certain her crampons were secure. He didn't want her to leave, but she had to. She'd insisted on writing her address and phone number down for him. He didn't really need them. He could find her anywhere through their mate bond.

"I guess it's time," she said. "I wish we could stay together."

"Soon," Jed promised. He held her pack so she could slide her arms through its straps.

"Yes," Terin said. "We need to do this right. Let's make certain we have our story straight."

Alice nodded. "It's easy enough because it's close to the truth. I camped last night in the little meadow across the creek. Spent a bunch of today hunting for Brent. Then you guys found me and told me you'd taken him to the hospital. I high-tailed it out of here."

"Perfect," Bron said approvingly. "By the way, I'm walking you to your car. We talked about it and none of us wanted you to go by yourself."

"You don't have to—" Alice began.

"It's not up for discussion," Jed interrupted. "Terin and I will wait about an hour. It will take that long to clean the cabin and get everything loaded onto the horses. Lon Chaney knows what we are. He's one of the few humans who appreciate us. He said one day he'll make a movie about shifters. Crazy drunk that he is, I believe him."

"I hadn't even thought about the horses since last night." Alice looked around. "Where are they?"

"There's a small barn about a quarter mile up the trail," Terin said. "Good thing too. If they weren't locked up, they would've turned into mountain lion fodder."

"Be careful." Jed brushed her forehead with his lips. "If you run into any problems, Bron will let us know."

She grinned. "I've been taking care of myself for a long time. I'm sure I could make it to my car by myself. The mountain lion was my own fault. I ran off halfcocked like a mad thing. I know better. If I'd had my things and my axe, I would've killed it."

"Yes, but you're not alone anymore. In fact, you'll never be alone again." Jed beckoned to Terin and Bron. They formed a circle around her. At his nod, they spoke in unison. "We love you. We will care for you and protect you so long as any of us shall live."

He swatted her on the butt. "Now get going. It'll be nearly dark before you and Bron get to your car."

"I'll wait for you in the Glacier Lodge parking lot once she leaves. I can get the horse trailer ready. We unhooked it before we drove the Hunter to Bishop." Bron punched Jed's arm lightly, then turned to Alice. "Ready?" She nodded. "Sure you don't want me to carry your rucksack?"

"Don't be absurd. Let's go."

~

BRON TROTTED alongside her as they headed down the trail. "Tell me about yourself."

"Well, I'm a civil engineer. I work for a firm in the Orange County area designing roads and bridges. And I spend as much time as I can in the mountains." She turned her head and glanced at him. "You?"

He snorted. "You told me what you do for a living, but that doesn't say much about who you are. I'm an engineer too, but a different kind. I work for Lockheed designing airplanes."

"What about Terin? Are you two as old as Jed?"

"Terin works with Jed. He's a cameraman for Paramount. He's a little older than Jed. Now me—" Bron winked at her "—I'm the baby of the group."

"What exactly does that mean in years?"

"Not quite five hundred."

Alice shook her head. This would all take a bit of time to get used to.

"Yes, it will."

"Crap. You can read my thoughts too."

"Of course. As the mate bond grows and deepens, you'll be able to see into our minds as well. Tell me about you," he persisted. "What's important to Alice?"

She thought about his question. "Work, family, the mountains. Doing the right thing and treating people kindly." She shrugged. "It's a hard question to answer."

He smiled. "You did just fine."

"What's important to you?"

"Pack. It's center of my world. Everything else comes and goes. Pack remains forever."

The trail narrowed, and he dropped behind her. Even though she couldn't see him, the glow from his energy surrounded her, warming and nurturing her and making her glad she'd taken a chance for once in her life.

"Engineers can be a stodgy lot," she murmured.

"That we can." Laughter followed Bron's words and he swatted her lightly across the butt.

She made a grab for his hand, but he was too quick for her.

CHAPTER 8

$\mathcal{A}$lice floated down the trail. Her heart was so full, everything around her glowed. Whatever she looked at, from Big Pine Creek canyon to a magpie that flew by, took on magical overtones. The world was multifaceted and brimming with wonder. She laughed because she felt so good. No matter how impossible it might seem to her engineer-trained mind, she'd found her true love on the mountain with a bonus to boot.

She looked forward to getting to know Jed, Bron, and Terin. Three very special men. It would be wonderful if the four of them could roam the Sierras, with her lovers free to shift to their wolf forms at will. She hadn't really gotten a very good look at any of them shifted except Jed.

Alice grappled with new sensations deep inside, grateful Bron wasn't talking with her. Since he was privy to her thoughts, he probably understood her need for quiet time. She felt the mate bond. It formed a glowing center somewhere near the bottom of her breastbone. Her mind felt different too. More alive and vibrant. The prospect of learning to manipulate magic excited her. What a boon it would be at work if she could read people's minds.

She crossed the South Fork trail junction. The trail had given way to a road half a mile back, but she hadn't been sure it would be snow free, so she'd left her car at the lodge. True to Jed's prediction, light leached from the day. Still high from making love, she loped the rest of the way to Glacier Lodge with Bron right beside her. Alice couldn't wait for the next time him and Jed and Terin sank their cocks deep inside her. She shook her head in consternation.

In some circles, they'd call me a whore. Better keep my mouth shut.

She grinned. Keeping quiet would scarcely be a problem. A confirmed loner, she didn't really have any friends.

I do now. Three of them, her inner voice crowed.

"That you do. Way more than friends, actually." The road had widened as they neared the lodge. Bron walked by her side and draped an arm around her shoulder. He whistled. "Wow! Is that your car? I wondered about it when Terin and I came through here last night."

"Yup."

Alice grinned and dug her keys out of her pants pocket. He pried them out of her hand and unlocked the door. She chucked her rucksack in the back seat, took a slug of water, and then patted her 1932 Ford V8 Cabriolet. "It was a splurge, but I don't have much else to spend my money on."

He opened his arms. She stepped into them and hugged him back before turning her face up for a kiss. He teased her with his tongue before closing his lips over hers. Running his hands down her back, he pulled her tight against him. She felt his cock swell against her belly. Her heartbeat quickened.

He broke away from their kiss. "Yes, sweetling. I'd love to take you right here, but Jed says you need to leave."

"You're talking with him?"

"Uh-huh. Right now. He said to tell you we all love you."

A pleased warmth rose to her face. "I can't imagine my life without you—any of you. And I can hardly wait to see the three of you again."

He kissed the tip of her nose and let her go.

Alice slid into her car. She fiddled with the timing lever, throttle, and fuel mixture, delighted when the Ford started on her first try. That didn't happen often. She gave the engine a chance to warm up. A few more adjustments and she waved to Bron before easing out of the parking lot and down the Glacier Lodge Road.

It took her over an hour to get to the north end of Bishop where the hospital was. Alice hoped they'd let her in. It was probably well past visiting hours, plus she was dirty and scrungy. She slammed her forehead against her hand. She had clothes in the trunk. She'd forgotten all about them. Alice headed for the far end of the parking lot and used the car to shield her while she changed into a black skirt, pressed white blouse, and black cardigan. She shoved her feet into low-heeled pumps without bothering with stockings.

She dug a hairbrush out of the glove box and went to work on her tangled locks. It took her about half an hour, but at least she felt presentable when she locked the Ford and strode toward the front doors of the hospital. As she'd expected, they were locked. She read a small placard and walked around the building to the emergency entrance.

"May I help you?" A nurse wearing a starched uniform and perky cap barred her way. Blonde curls peeked from under the brim of her cap. The nurse's blue eyes didn't look particularly friendly.

"I certainly hope so." Alice smiled brightly. "A friend of

mine had a climbing accident yesterday. I was told some men dropped him off here—"

"Oh, him." The nurse rolled her eyes. "What a handful he's been. Come with me." She beckoned. "Maybe he'll settle down if he sees someone he knows."

Alice set her jaw. This wouldn't be easy. She'd always been honest—with everyone. What came next would not only require her to lie, but that she do so convincingly.

"Let me out of here, goddammit," a voice bellowed from nearby.

"Criminey, he's at it again," the nurse muttered. "Need to give him more sedative. Go on in." She pointed at a door. "He's strapped down. Can't hurt you."

Alice turned the knob and pushed the white door marked 1C open. Her eyes widened, and her mouth fell open. It was all she could do not to clap a hand over her nose. The room stank of stale sweat and urine. Brent was indeed strapped down. His torso was wrapped in a straight jacket. His legs were bare, with a leather shackle bucked around each ankle.

"Holy shit," she gasped.

It looked like he had a hard time focusing, but Brent's gaze finally settled on her. "Alice?" he croaked.

"Yes, it's me." Compassion flooded her. What had happened to him? This seemed much worse damage than a concussion would've caused. Brent might be a Hunter, but he'd been a good friend to her. She took a step closer to the bed.

His nose wrinkled. His head thrashed from side to side. "Phew. You smell like *them*." A crafty gleam lit his green eyes. "Come closer, Alice. Tell me all about it. What did the shifters talk you into? Did they fill your head—and your twat —with ideas?"

"I have no idea what you're talking about," she sputtered. Heat blasted from her neck to the top of her head, and she knew she must've turned bright red. "You're being vulgar. If you don't stop immediately, I'm leaving."

"No." He yanked against the restraints. "Don't leave. You have to tell them there's nothing wrong with me. I'm not crazy. Alice." A line of spittle dribbled from one corner of his mouth. "You have to tell them to let me go."

Pity warred with disgust. This was a side of Brent she'd not only never seen, but never even imagined existed. "I'm not certain that's safe. You're sure not acting like yourself. Maybe when you hit your head—"

"I am too normal," he shrieked. "I know what you did, you dirty little slut. You think I didn't notice when you flashed your tits my way and rubbed up against me. All you women are the same. Bitches in heat. You'll do anything to get a cock inside you." He jerked his head toward his crotch. "Well, hey, I have one too. If you get me out of here, I'll—"

"You're being disgusting. Stop that right now." Alice balled her hands into fists to keep from smashing one into his nose.

"Stop." He laughed hysterically. "Why should I? You finally got laid. I can smell it all over you. How was it with all of them, huh? Did you come? Hah! I'll bet you creamed your—"

Alice spun and shoved the door open. She choked back a sob and nearly ran headlong into the nurse.

"Didn't go well, huh?" The nurse eyed her.

Alice shook her head. The door snicked shut behind her. Her eyes flooded. "There's something terribly wrong with him. He accused me of— Well, of horrible things. Things no well-bred person ever talks about." She wiped her streaming eyes.

"You fucking bitch," sounded through the door. "Slut. Whore of Babylon."

The nurse shoved her head through the door. "You stop that this instant. If you don't I'll give you enough medicine, you won't wake up until next week. Do I make myself clear?"

She backed out of the room and blew out an exasperated breath. "Damned bastard wet himself again. At this rate, we should move him to the nursery."

"Um, I'll be leaving," Alice murmured. "I guess it was a mistake for me to come here. It's just we were mountain climbing together, and I thought he'd need a ride back to Los Angeles. We only brought one car."

The nurse laid a hand on her arm. "Don't take this too hard, hon. Sometimes head injuries push 'em over the edge. Maybe they're a little bit crazy to begin with. Who knows?"

"What are you going to do with him?"

"Doc's thinking about sending him to one of the state mental hospitals. Given what just happened, I'd say it's a done deal. You run along, hon. Try to forget all about this." She stopped. "I hope he wasn't a special fellow or anything." Her eyes pinched with concern. She patted Alice's arm.

"No. Nothing like that. We were only climbing buddies. I'm okay. It was just a shock to see him like that."

"All right, hon. You take care now. I'm going to rustle up a few male orderlies to clean him up—again."

Alice walked slowly to her car. She wished there were a way to talk with Jed and Bron and Terin. Brent had been an entirely different person: hostile and bitter. His sexual accusations still burned. Had he always thought her a whore? She sucked in a ragged breath and realized how tired she was. Alice nursed her engine to life and sat while it got warm enough to back the choke off.

Even though it wasn't exactly a planned item in her budget, she decided to buy herself dinner and a motel room for the night. She was too tired to drive all the way back to southern California. She hoped a motel would still be open, and would rent a room to a woman by herself.

CHAPTER 9

Week Later

Alice let herself into her modest house. She wandered to the kitchen to see what she could turn into supper. A week had passed with no sign of Jed. If it weren't for the warmth of the mate bond deep inside her, she might've thought she'd imagined everything that happened at Lon Chaney's cabin. Earlier that day, she'd called Paramount Studios to try to track Jed down. A friendly sounding secretary had said, "Mr. Starnes is still on vacation." Alice hadn't left a message. She didn't even know Bron's or Terin's last name to start hunting for them.

"I'll be damned if I'm going to chase them," she muttered, but her heart and her body ached for her wolf shifters. She dreamed about them every night, awakening with damp thighs and a pounding heart.

Her phone rang. She listened for a moment to make certain it was her ring. She had an eight party line. It was annoying because kids in the other households often listened in to the few conversations she had, but private telephone lines were exorbitantly expensive. She clumped into the hall and picked up the black receiver. "Hello."

"Hi, sweetheart. Did you miss me?"

Her hand closed hard around the receiver. Relief swooshed through her. "Jed. Where on earth have you been?"

"I'll take it that's a yes. We're close. Mind if we stop by?"

"How close? When?"

"Five minutes. We're at the pay phone on the corner."

The line went dead. Alice raced to the bathroom, pulled the pins out of her hair, and brushed it until it glowed. She heard footsteps on the porch stairs just about the time she set the brush down. Excitement thrumming through her, she loped into the front room and tugged the door open.

Jed, Terin, and Bron pushed inside. All three were grinning like court jesters. Someone kicked the door into place. Someone else pulled the curtains shut. Jed folded his arms around her and murmured, "I've missed you something fierce, sweetheart."

She clung to him, drinking in his feel and smell. He kissed her, and she opened herself to him, sucking hungrily on his tongue. Desire forked through her like a lightning bolt.

Bron tugged her out of Jed's arms and kissed her thoroughly. She was just getting used to his mouth on hers when Terin spun her to face him and kissed her too, sinking his tongue deep into her mouth. After an endless time, he released her.

"Better." A smile lit his timeless features. "Much better. We missed you."

Alice glanced from one to the other. "I missed all of you too. Where were you?"

"Making certain Brent ended up in the state hospital. He made some pretty ugly accusations about all of us," Terin said.

"I'd left my name with the doctor," Bron explained. "He called to see if I'd be willing to testify before a Judge."

"What'd you say?" Alice untangled herself from three sets of arms.

Bron shrugged. "I was under oath. I told the truth. That we'd found him unconscious and used horses to get him to our car."

She almost hated to ask, but she wanted to know. "Um, how was he?"

"I don't know. The court commitment process doesn't work like that. I never saw him."

Jed draped an arm around her, pulled her to him, and kissed her forehead. "How was he when you saw him?"

Alice shook her head. "Horrible. He was gross and disgusting and accused me of terrible things—"

"Ssht." Jed smoothed her hair out of her face. Taking handfuls, he pushed it over her shoulders. "It will be fine. I just thought we ought to lie low for a few days until this whole thing blew over. Brent will be in the mental hospital for years, if not forever. Once you go into those places, they never let you out."

"Don't feel too bad," Terin said. "Hunters are all a little crazy. If they weren't, they'd never fall for the whole chastity and obedience thing."

"He probably lusted after you all along." Jed quirked a brow. "When he figured out we'd had you in all the ways he wanted to, well, it probably finished the job that rock he landed on started."

She nodded, feeling sad. "I wanted to talk with you that night I saw him in the hospital."

"That's the first thing I'll teach you, then," Jed said. "How to reach me if I'm not right next to you."

"First thing after the more important stuff." Terin chortled.

Alice glanced around. "Maybe if we're really quiet. Lots of people are sitting out in their yards this time of night."

"The lady has a point." Jed grinned. "We'll be silent as church mice." He pulled her into his arms. "And then we'll all go out for an elaborate multi-course dinner to celebrate."

"After that, you'll come home with us." Terin smiled broadly. "We have a big house with thick walls."

"And an indoor pool to play in," Bron added.

Alice's eyes widened. "There probably won't be time for me to see it tonight, but where do you live?"

"In the Hollywood Hills. You'll love it." Bron's arms circled her from behind, sandwiching her between his body and Jed's. Two cocks prodded her, one in front, one behind. Alice's blood heated. Her nipples pebbled into points of sensation where they rubbed against Jed's chest. She rocked her hips. A flood of desire slicked her thighs.

"Hey, found the bedroom," Terin called softly. "This way."

Jed's eyes darkened with love and desire. She was coming to recognize that look. He let go of her. "Lead on. I can't wait."

Terin was already naked when Alice got there. His cock jutted upward, curved against his stomach. He patted it. "We've spent a lot of time this last week talking about you and jacking off. I'm ready for the real thing."

Jed laughed softly. "Love your enthusiasm."

"How about mine?" Bron's clothes joined Terin's in a heap on a chair.

"Gee," Alice eyed both hard ons. "I'm starting to feel over-dressed here." She reached for the buttons on the plain cotton blouse she'd worn to work, but Jed batted her hands away.

"Let me." He undid her blouse and moved it off her shoulders, then reached around and unclasped her bra. Jed sucked in a breath. "You are so beautiful."

He filled his hands with her breasts and bent forward to

settle his mouth over hers. His tongue pushed insistently against her lips. Alice opened her mouth and took him inside. Her tongue sparred with his. His fingers worked her nipples, and they hardened still more beneath his touch. Two bodies closed on either side of her. Two more erections jutted into her sides. She moved her mouth away from Jed and kissed first Bron, then Terin.

She reached for the hooks on her skirt. It fell to the floor. Someone pushed her panties down her hips. Alice's breath caught in her throat. She was so aroused, it was all she could do to keep breathing. Jed undid his pants, stepped out of them, and guided her to the bed.

"I've dreamed of feeling you around me," he said, his voice husky with passion. "We all have." He sat so his back was against the wall and his legs were stretched out in front of him. "Come sit on me, sweetheart, I can't wait any longer."

Alice knelt on her bed and straddled Jed's lap. He sank into her, groaning his delight. Her back arched like a bow. Delight thrummed through her, heating her blood. Terin settled behind her and wrapped his arms around her. Capturing a breast in each hand, he twirled her nipples into exquisite points of delight. His hard on surged against her back where he rubbed himself against her. Bron half stood, half knelt on the bed, his erection at mouth level.

She wrapped a hand around his shaft and guided him inside her mouth, licking, nibbling, and kissing. Jed settled his hands on her hips. He set a rhythm and drove himself into her. The tension in his body gave him away. She knew he had to be close. Between the cock in her pussy, the one in her mouth, and the one pressing into the small of her back, the pleasure was so intense, she wanted to scream her joy to the world. Alice stifled the cry that wanted out. The walls were too thin. Last thing she needed were nosy neighbors who'd watched three men enter her house, followed by the unmistakable sounds of lovemaking.

The mate bond burned hot inside her. Jed pulled almost all the way out and slammed himself home. She tightened her muscles around him, and a climax began deep in her belly. Terin's cock bucked against her back, followed by flashes of heat. Semen ran down her butt. Bron pulled out of her mouth and jacked himself hard with his hand. Watching him come drove her over the edge. Her climax roared out of her. She bit down on her hand to muffle her cries. Jed's cock juddered inside her over and over.

"Yes," he murmured. "Oh, my God, yes."

Alice collapsed on top of him before rolling to one side. Terin and Bron crowded close. Alice wriggled her hips.

"I'd say the lady needs to come again," Jed said. "Who wants to do the honors?"

Terin rearranged his body so he could close his mouth over her clit. Bron's fingers plumbed her. Jed sucked her nipples. Alice buried her hands in Terin's hair and drove her pussy against his face. "She's close," Bron said, "suck harder."

Alice's orgasm rocked her to her core. She came so hard her body, fondled by the three men who loved her, was the only thing in the world. Before she completely quit spasming, Bron turned her over and tugged her onto her hands and knees just before he sank his cock deep inside her.

She gave herself up to pure sensation. Jed and Terin positioned themselves on their knees so their cocks were next to her mouth. She sucked first one, then the other, then back again, crazy with wanting both of them, all of them.

Bron gripped her hips hard. His cock shuddered inside her. She felt the heat of his passion and the ecstasy of his release. At first it confused her, and then she understood she was starting to see into their minds. His fingers reached around and rubbed her sensitive nub hard. He kept on stroking her, cock just as hard as before he'd come. She dissolved into another climax. The air shimmered in multi-hued tones.

"I think I've died and gone to heaven," she said.

"I'd wait on that assessment until after I'm done." Terin grinned at her and moved off the bed.

Bron pulled out of her. Terin lifted her from the bed. He led her to a straight-backed chair and sat on it, then faced her away from him, and drew her down atop his curving erection. His hands on her hips set a rhythm.

"I've dreamed of being inside you again," he said. "Damn, if the three of us didn't drive each other crazy with describing how you felt and smelled and looked when you came."

Jed and Bron moved close, one on either side. Jed's cock was still rock hard. He nudged it against her mouth. She opened to take him in. Bron insinuated his body between them, knelt on the floor and rubbed her clit with one hand and a nipple with the other. She sucked and licked Jed while Terin pushed his cock firmly inside her. Bron's fingers gripped her clit.

"She's almost there," he murmured. "Go for it, guys."

Jed's cock bucked in her hand. Salty semen spurted into her mouth. It tasted wonderful. She swallowed and sucked hard for more. Terin's cock swelled inside her. Bron rubbed harder. Alice wouldn't have thought it possible, but another climax began deep in her belly. It rioted through her just as she felt Terin judder again and again. Gasping for air, she fell back against his body.

"Now that was worth waiting for," she said when she could talk again.

Jed kissed her tenderly. "No, sweetheart. You were worth waiting for." He bent to collect his clothes. "How about it, guys. Who's up for dinner?"

"We are." Terin and Bron laughed, but kept their voices low.

"Yeah, that was great," Terin said. "I won't be up for much of anything except dinner for at least an hour."

"Only an hour?" Alice joined their laughter. "That was a hell of an appetizer."

~

JED ORDERED another bottle of Cabernet and gazed fondly at his pack. The Italian restaurant had been a perfect choice. It was dark inside, so dark it was impossible to read the menus without holding them next to the candle that sat atop each table. They were in a private corner booth where they could snuggle and kiss as they wished.

Happiness made his heart light. He still couldn't believe their pack had a mate. It had been so long, he'd given up hope. And what a mate. Alice was a hell of a woman. Strong, sure of herself, and with an animal magnetism to rival their own. He couldn't wait until the babies started coming.

Alice held up her glass. "Could I have a little more?"

"Of course." Terin reached across Jed for the bottle and poured.

She took another mouthful of a lasagna-esque dish liberally spiced with basil, tarragon, and thyme and reached for a slice of garlic bread. "Mmm. What a great choice. The food is exquisite."

"That's because you worked up an appetite." Bron winked at her.

"I'd been working on one for the entire week." She grinned at him. "When I wasn't worried sick I'd never see you guys again."

Jed wrapped an arm around her shoulders and squeezed lightly. "We wanted to call you, but the cops can check phone records. We didn't want to implicate you in case something went wrong." He helped himself to a bite off her plate. His own was empty, but he'd had enough to eat. "Save room for dessert. They make a lemon cream cake that's to die for."

Alice glanced at her watch and raised her eyebrows. "Oh my. How'd it get to be nine o'clock already? I need to be up at five. We're going to have to skip that dessert."

Jed nuzzled her neck. Sitting on her other side, Bron stroked her leg.

"Maybe you could take a sick day." Jed smiled hopefully.

Alice made shooing motions with both hands and nudged the two shifters an inch or so away. "Nope. Not the way we're starting this. My job is important to me. It's part of who I am."

"I understand." Jed pushed a strand of hair over her shoulder. "We want you to be happy."

Terin gazed at her from his spot across the table. He moved forward so his knees bumped against hers. "Better. I like it when at least part of me is touching you."

"We'll leave soon, so you can get some sleep before you have to go to work tomorrow." Warmth gleamed from Bron's dark eyes.

"Yes but we'll take you to our house," Jed said. "I can drop you off at work tomorrow—"

Alice held up a hand, and furrowed her brow in thought. "I've had a little too much wine to think clearly, but how about this? Take me home tonight. Give me your address. I won't have time to get much together tonight, but tomorrow after work, I'll go home, gather a few things, and then I'll come and visit for a few days."

"We think you should move in," the three shifters said almost in unison.

She snorted. "You've seen what a bitch I can be. Let's experiment. If it turns out well, we'll make the living arrangement permanent." Her eyes softened, moving to each man in turn. "I want this to work. The last week's been a special kind of hell, not knowing where you were or if I'd ever see you again." She blinked furiously and brushed away a tear that glistened on one cheek.

Jed exchanged glances with Bron and Terin. "No hurry here. Everything will unfold in its own time. Let the mate bond work its magic. I love you." He turned his head and brushed her lips with his in the gentlest of kisses. Bron did the same.

"Hey," Terin protested. "I feel left out." He got out of his seat, shoved between Bron and Alice, and kissed her too, before straightening.

Alice scrubbed at tears on both cheeks. Her green eyes shone with happiness. "I'm falling in love with all of you. Thanks for respecting what I need."

"We're pack," Jed said solemnly.

"Yes," Terin chimed in. "We listen to one another."

Bron laid a hand on her leg. "We wouldn't be much of a family if we ran roughshod over one another's wishes."

"Here." Alice scrabbled in her handbag and drew out a crumpled bank deposit slip and a pen. She handed them to Jed. "Write your address and phone number down for me. While we're at it—" she skewered Bron and Terin with her green gaze "—what are your last names?"

"We all use Starnes," Bron replied. "It makes the story that we're brothers more credible."

Jed scrawled something on the paper and handed it back to Alice along with her pen. "What time should we expect you tomorrow night?"

She paused for a beat. "Probably around six thirty. Maybe seven. Why?"

Feral protectiveness surged through him, and he gripped her hand. "Because you're ours, and we take care of what belongs to us. If you're any later than seven, we'll come hunting for you."

She winked broadly before snuggling closer. "I like that. I could get used to being cared about. So long as you're not heavy-handed about it."

"Never." He nuzzled her neck.

Bron and Terin formed a circle around her. "We'll love you and care for you forever," Jed declared, his voice solemn. Fueled by the mate bond, emotion rocked him to his core. He wondered how he'd be able to walk away from Alice when they left her at her doorstep. But he'd figure it out. Her happiness trumped everything. Making her happy, and keeping her that way, had become a cornerstone of his existence.

"You're part of our pack now," Bron added.

"A very welcome part." Terin bent and kissed the top of her head.

"It's not going to be easy to leave you boys tonight," Alice murmured, "but I have to go home and get some sleep."

Jed exchanged glances with his lieutenants. They understood. Together, they helped Alice to her feet and walked out of the restaurant and into a star-studded night.

EPILOGUE

Two months later

Alice nosed the Ford Cabriolet higher into the Hollywood Hills. She couldn't erase the grin from her face. The last couple of months had been the happiest of her life. She turned into Jed's driveway, pulled off into the gravel beside the garage, and set her parking brake.

"Anybody home?"

She projected her mind voice. It was fun to talk that way, especially when they were in a crowd and she wanted to say something private. There were gradations. She could project a general question to her three shifter mates like she'd just done, or she could hold a more personal conversation with just one of them.

No one answered, so she switched to a different telepathic frequency, one that would carry much farther. *"Jed?"*

"Terin and I are on our way, sweetheart. Home in fifteen."

"Love you."

"You too, darling."

She grabbed her overflowing briefcase off the passenger

seat and let herself into the house. The first time she'd seen it, it had taken the better part of an hour to pull her eyes back into their sockets. The six thousand square foot Neo-Grecian mansion had columns, fountains, and flower gardens. Three above-ground floors housed a resplendent collection of priceless antiques. And the basement even had an indoor pool.

Jed had confided that most of the paintings, rugs, sculptures, crystal, and silver weren't truly antiques, since either he or Bron or Terin had purchased them when they were new and simply hung onto them. Alice ran her hand over shiny mahogany tables and picked up a delicate crystal hummingbird. She held it up to a window, delighted when it reflected all the colors of the rainbow. Feeling foolish, she put it down and mounted polished hardwood stairs to her room on the top floor. Its leaded glass windows opened onto a small balcony directly over a rose garden. The scent from the flowers was heady and overpowering on warm spring nights. The men had given her a choice of rooms. The minute she'd seen this one with its sloping ceilings and graceful Louis the Fifteenth furniture, she'd fallen in love.

One end of the second floor housed a huge bedroom with a gigantic bed. They played and slept there, but each of them had a room like hers for quiet time.

She dropped her briefcase on the chair next to her desk and wondered if she had time for a quick dip in the pool before the men came home. Bron didn't usually get home much before seven. She'd come to respect his analytical skills. They'd sat with their heads bent over more than one engineering design problem.

Alice got out of her work clothes and hung them in the oversized closet. She kicked off her shoes and stripped off her underthings, smiling to herself. She needed to buy more clothes. The closet was barely a quarter full. She'd always watched her money closely—and she still did. Jed and the others had reassured her she could have whatever she wanted, but old habits died hard. Besides, she didn't need a lot of things to make her happy.

The mate bond glowed behind her breastbone. She laid a hand over it. Joy filled her. Each man held a special place in her heart. "The shifter magic ain't too shabby, either," she murmured and then laughed.

Alice grabbed a large, lavender Turkish towel and wound it around herself. Her hair was pinned up in a bun, so she just left it. Humming to herself, she walked down three flights of stairs and pushed open the door to the indoor pool. It was damp and steamy and smelled incredible from the potted herbs and plants the men grew there. Jed had an architectural background. He'd designed the pool to look like it was in the middle of a South American jungle with greenery growing so near the water's edge, flowers and leaves floated on its surface. The effect was so true-to-life, she'd kept an eye out for piranha her first few swims.

Alice chucked her towel on a chaise lounge and jumped into the deep end of the pool. The water was perfect. The shifters employed some kind of magic to keep it clean and the water temperature a brisk seventy degrees. Algae clinging to the plants probably helped clean the water too. She flipped over onto her stomach and swam laps. She'd always loved water. To be able to swim whenever she wanted was icing on the cake.

"Sweetheart!"

Jed cannonballed into the pool, followed by Terin. They closed on her and kissed her thoroughly. At first, Jed wrapped his arms around her from the front and Terin from the back. Then they switched. Fingers tweaked her nipples. Both men were hard, and their erections prodded her body. Alice's breath hitched. No matter how many times she and her shifters made love, she always wanted more.

Jed probed between her legs with nimble fingers. She twisted away from him and dove under the water. When she surfaced, she stroked hard for the far side of the pool. Jed and Terin followed.

"Come back, sweetheart," Jed cried. "We've barely begun."

She heaved herself onto the side of the pool. "We promised Bron we'd wait for him."

"So we did." Terin nodded. He jumped out of the water and sat next to her, cock jutting out from his body. He wrapped a hand around himself, stroking lightly.

"Thanks for the reminder." Jed pulled himself out of the water and sat on her other side. He rubbed his erection and looked wistfully at her. "I forget everything when you're close like this."

"Close and naked." Terin grinned.

"What time is it?" Alice looked at the men.

"Maybe six-thirty," Jed answered. "Bron will be home soon."

"Thank God." Terin groaned. He stroked his shaft a couple more times and dove back into the pool.

"Want to swim a little more?" Jed traced the line of her breasts with his index finger. Hunger radiated from the depths of his eyes. He cupped the side of her face with his hand and turned it so he could kiss her.

Alice's nipples stiffened. Her core fired with need. Before desire swamped her, she pulled away. "Sure. It's a great diversion. Then we can all clean up. By the time we're done, Bron will be home."

She slipped back into the pool and swam to its far end, passing Terin along the way. The three of them did a few more laps, and then headed for the enormous Grecian tub next to their shared bedroom on the second floor. Jed flipped the taps. Water flowed into the sunken tub from goddesses holding urns. Green-veined Italian marble darkened as water splashed on it.

She'd just stepped into the tub, when the bathroom door opened and Bron burst in. He rubbed his hands together. "Excellent. You really did wait for me. I didn't think you would."

Jed elbowed him in the side. "You can thank Alice. Terin and I would've started the party without you."

"Thanks, buddy. I'll remember that."

"Maybe when we've had Alice for, oh, fifty years, we'll be able to exercise a bit more restraint." Terin winked at him. "One of the benefits of the mate bond is she'll live a long time." He made an impatient hand gesture. "Come on, fellow, get out of your clothes."

"Anxious to see my awesome physique?"

"Nope. Just trying to be true to what we promised." He moved down the steps and into the steaming water. Jed catapulted over the edge and took Alice in his arms. He closed his mouth over hers and licked between her lips. She opened her mouth and wound her arms around him. The same incredible scent that had snared her in Lon Chaney's cabin rose from all three shifters. It was spicy and exotic and impossible to resist. The men had told her it was their pheromones and that she had them too.

Terin held her from behind. He shoved his hands between her and Jed's bodies and filled them with her breasts. His erection pushed against her butt. Jed's moved against her stomach. Bron waded up next to them and fitted his body to her side. Already fully hard, his cock pushed against her hipbone. She broke away from her kiss with Jed and kissed Bron. Her body ached for all of them. Their group sex games had grown even more exciting now than they'd been at the beginning, when she didn't know much.

Each man's body was a little different. Jed liked being in her mouth. Terin and Bron preferred her pussy. Their skin felt heavenly under her fingertips. She moved one of her arms from around Jed and wrapped it behind Bron. It never mattered who did what to whom first. By the time they were done, everyone was always satiated.

Jed stepped back and picked up a washcloth. He dipped it in the water and ran it down her front. "Let's pretend she's a goddess—" he grinned wickedly "—and we're all her sex slaves."

"Pretend?" She eyed him with mock severity. "I am a goddess. Your goddess and don't you ever forget it." Her mouth was dry with longing. "Speaking of which, Jed may be the pack alpha, but you're all my alphas."

"Hear that?" Bron elbowed Terin.

"I do, indeed," Terin shot back. "And I like it. A lot."

"Just so long as you don't get ideas outside this room." Jed tried to sound fierce, but he ruined the effect by breaking into gales of laughter.

Bron and Terin grabbed terrycloth squares of their own. One worked on her back, one on her legs. Then they traded with Jed who reluctantly gave up her breasts and belly. They stood closer than they had to so their cocks pushed against her.

Alice spun away. "First one who can make me come without touching my pussy gets to fuck me." She grinned lasciviously at the men. It wasn't really fair, she was so hot, she'd come practically the minute one of them suckled her nipples, but she wasn't about to tell them that.

"You mean gets to fuck you, first," Jed corrected.

She laughed. "You've turned me into a hussy and you know what? I love it. Come on." She crooked a finger at them.

Bron dove for her nipples. He pressed her breasts together and tongued both at once, his tongue lashing from one to the other. Jed ran a finger down the middle of her back and settled it teasingly between her legs, but not inside her. He proceeded to move in small, playful circles. Terin knelt in the water, pushed her legs apart, and blew on her exposed nub.

Her body convulsed. She wanted Terin's mouth on her. She wanted Jed's fingers inside, but she'd made the rules. Her hips thrust forward. She buried her hands in Terin's hair and tried to jam her pussy against his mouth, but he kept an angstrom of distance between his wonderfully hot breath and her throbbing center. And then it didn't matter. Her climax spewed out. The spasms just kept rolling through her. Once she started coming, all bets were off. Terin sucked her clit. Jed jammed his fingers inside her. Bron sucked hard on her nipples.

"Look at her," Jed said. "She's all rosy. Tell us, sweetheart, which of us won?"

"You all cheated." She gasped when she could talk again.

"Maybe, but only after you started coming." Terin rose to his feet and kissed her. The taste of herself on his lips made her want to crawl up his body and impale herself on his cock.

"How about we move this to the bed?" Jed took her hand and led her to the steps at the end of the tub. He wrapped her blushing body in a towel and grabbed one for himself.

Alice couldn't get to the bed fast enough. She tossed her wet towel over a chair and jumped onto the middle of the bed. Her climax hadn't made a dent in her desire. She wanted all three of those cocks buried to the hilt in her body. She spread her legs and plunged two fingers into her pussy. The guys loved to see her touch herself. It drove them half mad with desire.

Jed pushed her hand away and knelt between her legs. He wrapped a hand around his shaft and groaned as he sank inside her. Bron and Terin knelt on each side of her. She took Bron into her mouth and worked Terin with her hand. Then she switched. They often started this way.

Jed drove into her. She pulled her legs up and wrapped them around his body. Terin rubbed her nipples. Bron rubbed her clit. Alice could barely stand it. She came just before she felt Jed release inside her. Her hand tightened on Bron, her mouth on Terin.

Jed moved aside. Terin turned her over. She pushed to her hands and knees. He sank inside her. Bron positioned himself in front of her, and she bent her head to take him into her mouth. He wrapped his hands around her head and drove himself into her. Jed moved in from the side. He lay on his back and tugged her body down a little so he could suck her clit.

Bron came first. She felt the tension build in his ridged flesh, and then he spurted hard into her mouth. Jed must've felt Bron's release because he sucked harder. Terin fucked her faster, and the world fell away. She came hard, bucking between two cocks and Jed's magical tongue.

Alice gasped for breath, but the room still spun crazily. Sex with her shifter pack was just about the best thing in the world. Bron abandoned her mouth. Terin pulled out of her body. Hands turned her over. Bron jacked his half hard cock. It didn't take much encouragement before it was engorged and pressing against her pussy lips. She opened herself to him and reached for Terin and Jed.

They moved to either side of her and their cocks settled into her hands. She stroked their shafts while Bron plumbed her. Terin and Jed tweaked her nipples and her clit. Alice felt another climax build deep in her belly. Her orgasms just got better and better. The first one barely took the edge off. It took several before she could get sex out of her mind and focus on something else.

Her muscles clenched around Bron. She thrust her hips against him. Terin laid a finger on either side of her clit and twirled it. Alice shrieked with delight. Her body turned to molten heat and she came again.

"Yes, darling, that's it. I'm right behind you." Bron moved faster and faster. His high pitched yelp as he juddered inside her warmed her soul.

When she could breathe again, she tweaked the two cocks still in her hands. "How about it? Anyone for thirds? Or was that fourths?"

Jed laughed. "I'm for dinner."

"Me too." Terin moved off the bed. "I could come again, but maybe we should save something for later."

Alice slithered off the bed. "I'm going to rinse off in the tub."

"Sounds like a grand idea." Jed padded after her. "Where do you want to go for dinner?"

She smiled at him, feeling warm and wonderful and over-flowing with love. "Could we go back to the Italian place?"

"Anything you want, sweetheart." He folded her into his arms and kissed her.

Bron and Terin joined them. Not to be outdone, they hugged and kissed her too.

"Do you suppose you're ready to put your house on the market?" Bron asked.

"Or at least rent it out?" Jed added. "Not that we need the money, but it's not in the greatest neighborhood, and it's not a good idea to let it sit empty."

Well, am I ready to do that?

Alice didn't waste much time soul-searching. Living with

Jed and his lieutenants had been better than her wildest dreams. She couldn't imagine her life without them. "Why don't we sell it?" She furled a brow at Jed. "While we're at it, how about that marriage proposal you tossed my way at the cabin."

A brilliant smile lit his face. "Sweetheart, I thought you'd never ask."

Alice clapped her hands together. "Excellent! Right after the ceremony, I want us all to go mountain climbing."

"It will be like a honeymoon." Bron grinned.

"Yes," Terin added, "for all of us."

"Wolves too," she said. "I want a chance to get to know them better."

"Maybe—" Jed furrowed his brow as he mulled it over "—if we went to the Canadian Rockies it would be deserted enough we could risk it."

"Excellent idea," Bron chimed in. "We have clan there. We could run with them."

"Perfect. I'll get to meet more of you." She smiled at all of them and stepped into the water. Love for her men filled her and ran over. Behind her breastbone, the mate bond shone warmer than any sun.

WOLF CLAN SHIFTERS continues in Megan's Mates. You'll find all the characters from Alice's Alphas, plus two shifters from the clan's Canadian kin and the lucky woman who ends up their mate. A sample chapter follows.

ABOUT THE AUTHOR

Ann Gimpel is a national bestselling author. A lifelong aficionado of the unusual, she began writing speculative fiction a few years ago. Since then her short fiction has appeared in a number of webzines and anthologies. Her longer books run the gamut from urban fantasy to paranormal romance. Once upon a time, she nurtured clients. Now she nurtures dark, gritty fantasy stories that push hard against reality. When she's not writing, she's in the backcountry getting down and dirty with her camera. She's published over 50 books to date, with several more planned for 2018 and beyond. A husband, grown children, grandchildren and wolf hybrids round out her family.

Keep up with her at www.anngimpel.com or http://anngimpel.blogspot.com

If you enjoyed what you read, get in line for special offers and pre-release special reads. Sign up for Ann's newsletter on her website or her blog.

MEGAN'S MATES

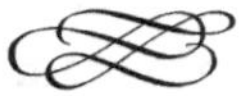

utumn, 1936

The swish of tires on wet pavement drove Megan deeper into the shadows of a band of oak trees. She pulled her black wool cloak tighter against her body and set her teeth to keep them from chattering. Maybe running away from the Garden of Eden cult hadn't been such a hot idea, but staying didn't work either. Not after what she'd witnessed last night.

When she'd joined the group two years ago, they'd been warm and welcoming. The rituals were a bit risqué, but harmless all in all. She squeezed her eyes shut to block out the image of a cheering mob that had segued from chanting while scantily clad to blood sacrifice. Exposing her body was one thing, a thirst for human blood quite another...

She pried her eyes open. No one would save her except herself, and there wasn't much she could do by playing ostrich. Escape was essential. The only thing that mattered. Never mind she'd be walking away from what little she owned since her things were in one of the cult's many apartments.

Megan took another step backward. One boot sank into

sticky mud, and cold water ran into it. Reality hit home and terrified her. She couldn't go back to work. Nearly everyone she knew at the insurance exchange was related to the cult in some way. Or to another similar group. Occult fervor had risen during the twenties in the wake of World War I. By the middle of the nineteen thirties, it had a well-established toehold. Fascination with the supernatural ran high and had grown like an out-of-control weed. Most spiritual cults were rooted in the States, but it hadn't taken long before Canadians picked up the banner, enthralled by the unseen world.

Despite Megan's best efforts, shudders racked her body, and her teeth banged against one another uncontrollably. October in Calgary meant the air was dry and crisp. She'd seen frost on the roofs this morning. Tonight would likely be another freeze. It didn't take much of an imagination to realize winter would set in soon.

Somehow, she'd sat at her desk all day. When co-workers commented she seemed subdued, she'd just said she wasn't feeling well. It was the only way she'd gotten out of mandatory attendance at tonight's cult meeting. Midday, she'd slipped out of the office and stopped by the bank. Closing her account would've engendered suspicion, so she'd withdrawn two hundred dollars, half of what she had saved. Even that earned her a stern lecture from one of the bank vice presidents. Likely afraid she'd fallen for some scam, he drew her into a side office, intent on discovering why she needed such a vast sum of money. Megan rolled her eyes at the memory. She'd fabricated a story about a mythical aunt who had unexpected medical bills.

"Yes, and I'm wasting precious time standing here," she muttered, the words barely discernable against her chattering teeth. If she was going to follow through with the plan she'd hatched during the day, she needed to be out of town and well-hidden before someone looked for her. If she got really lucky, that wouldn't be until after she didn't show up for work tomorrow.

Aw crap! They might send someone to my place tonight to see if I need anything.

That last thought galvanized her into action. Megan broke into a shambling trot and ducked into a coffee shop. She needed something hot to drink, and then she'd head for the train station and catch the evening express north toward Edmonton.

"Looking pretty wet there, hon." A smiling waitress hustled over to her. "We're closing soon, but I can get you some soup."

"Just coffee," Megan managed. "And I promise I'll drink it fast."

The waitress, a buxom blonde with gray roots, cocked her head to one side. "You okay, sweetie?" Her brown eyes flickered kindly.

"Fine." She dug a nickel out of a pocket. "Here's for the coffee. I like it black."

The waitress frowned and then shrugged. "It's six cents now, but seeing as how we're just going to toss what's left in the pot, keep your money. Looks as if you need it worse than we do."

Tears threatened at the woman's unexpected thoughtfulness. Megan blinked them back and murmured, "Thank you." She sank into a red leather padded chair at the counter and waited while the waitress poured steaming liquid into a heavy, white ceramic mug. The heated crockery felt heavenly when she cradled it between her hands. The coffee burned her tongue, but the jolt from the caffeine was instantaneous and welcome.

Megan glanced at her watch. How had it gotten to be nine p.m.? Her train left in an hour. The station was a thirty minute walk, and she needed time to purchase a ticket once she got there. She didn't have extra money to waste on streetcars or taxis. Setting her cup down, she nodded at the waitress and hurried out of the café. The streets weren't exactly deserted, so she pulled the sodden wool of her cloak's hood over her bright hair. She didn't want to have to explain why she hadn't been at the meeting if anyone recognized her. After all, her excuse had been she was too sick to leave her home that night, and it would be blown to hell if anyone spotted her wandering around in marginal weather.

Stop that! She lectured herself. *Everyone else is at cult head-quarters. No one's out and about who might recognize me.*

Brave words. Too bad I don't believe them.

Her heart thudded so hard, she was afraid everyone she passed could hear it. Megan counted off blocks as she walked through the heart of Calgary's business district. Her wet sock squished in her boot. She wished she had time to take it off and wring it out. Another café, this one advertising it stayed open until ten, looked inviting, but she walked on by.

I'll take care of my sock problem at the station. I'm cutting the timing close as it is.

Megan felt ill. The coffee she'd welcomed going down burned her stomach like acid. If she met up with anyone from the cult at the train station, she'd be finished. Cult members signed on for life. There weren't any early out clauses that she knew of. A tear dripped down one cheek; she brushed it aside. No point feeling sorry for herself. She'd made a bad decision and didn't have a fallback position. No family to run home to —or call for help. They'd all died in the flu epidemic of 1918. She'd been seven at the time and had ended up in the Calgary orphanage.

"Even if I had relatives," she mumbled, "they'd be the last place I'd go. Wouldn't want to implicate them." There hadn't been anything truly wrong with the orphanage, but there hadn't been much right there, either. Megan understood perfectly why she'd been so attracted to the cult. For the first time in her twenty-five years, she felt as if she belonged some-where. Like she had a family.

What a joke! Megan castigated herself for being a fool, and a gullible one at that, and then gave it up for wasted effort.

The station lights shone through ground fog that had misted out of nowhere during her flight across town. A few more steps and she pushed the door open, walking into warmth so welcome it took her breath away. She didn't realize how cold she'd become. Not just body-cold. Her spirit was frozen to the core of her soul.

Megan gazed around the station. A few people milled about, but not many. Resolute now that she was here, she marched to an open ticket counter and said, "Edmonton, please. Economy coach."

The man didn't bother to look up. "How many?" In his fifties or sixties, he was rail thin with sparse, gray hair.

"Just me."

"Name?"

"Megan Galen."

His fingers shook as he wrote out her ticket. "That'll be a dollar-fifty, miss."

"Oh." She bit her lower lip and fished in her handbag.

He glanced at her, rheumy blue eyes shrewd. "You got a problem with that?"

Megan swallowed hard. It went against the grain, but she spoke up for herself. "Since you asked, yes I do. I don't have much, and I thought the advertised fare was a dollar. I, um, called today and asked about it."

He shrugged. "You got a buck?" She held it up so he could see. "Okay, missy. Here's your ticket." He stamped it and held it out to her, but Megan was so nonplussed he'd tried to over-charge her, she didn't reach for it.

"Ain't you going to take your ticket?" He sounded annoyed.

"Yeah, sure." She pushed her money under the bars and took the ticket.

"Gate seven. She boards in twenty minutes."

Megan scuttled away, not wanting to deal with the clerk who'd tried to cheat her. If she wouldn't have said anything, he would've pocketed the extra fifty cents. Outrage flooded her and left a bitter taste at the back of her mouth. Someone really should report him.

Yes, someone should, but not me. The last thing I need is to draw attention to myself.

Following the signs, she settled in to wait near where the train would come and bent to unlace her boot. Her sock had soaked up most of the water. She wrung out what she could and put it back on before the wool could cool off and become clammy. Some strands of her white-blonde hair had escaped from beneath her hood. She tucked them back out of sight and drew in a shuddery breath. Fifteen more minutes and she'd be safe on the train. Well, maybe safe, though it seemed unlikely she'd run into any Garden of Edeners on the night train to Edmonton.

She'd studied maps during the day and decided to get off at Red Deer. Buying a ticket all the way to Edmonton was a hedge in case anyone tried to find out where she'd gone. From Red Deer, hopefully she could hitch a ride west into some of the smaller communities dotting the Rockies. Maybe, if she was really lucky, she could land a job before her money ran out. Insofar as she knew, cult activities were limited outside major cities.

Wonder how much trouble they're going to go to in order to find me?

The loudspeaker announced her train. After a final, furtive glance around the station, Megan strode toward the door and out onto the platform. The steam engine's headlamp lit the night. With a whoosh and a roar, the train clattered to a halt. She waited until a flood of travelers disembarked, climbed the steps, and found her way to a nearly deserted coach.

Her seat was soft and the train car warm. Her eyelids grew heavy before the train even pulled out of the station. Megan pinched her hands. Sleeping, at least until they got underway, wasn't an option. She had to stay alert and keep an eye on the few passengers entering her car.

It wasn't easy. She'd barely slept the night before as her mind replayed the horror of a man she'd known and respected chopping off two of his fingers while lost in cult-driven zeal. If it had just been him, acting by himself, it might've been one thing, but hundreds of other cult members were screeching, cheering, and egging him on. They'd put his fingers into a brass bowl and used the blood to try to lure a spirit guide.

When their efforts didn't seem to be working, the man twisted and plunged his knife into the nearest bystander, a woman Megan knew from work, screeching, "We need more blood."

The woman fell to the floor shrieking and clutching a belly spewing blood. Rather than summoning aid, the other cult members sank into a pitched argument about the trouble they'd get into if anyone found out.

Horrified and disbelieving—and with the woman's piteous cries for help echoing in her ears—Megan excused herself, barely making it to the ladies' room before her stomach rebelled. She hadn't returned, but the cult was so high on bloodlust, she figured no one noticed her absence. She'd placed an anonymous call to the Police from a corner pay phone before scurrying home and locking her doors.

Showing up at work today, so she could buy herself enough time to flee, had taken every shred of strength she possessed. As the minutes ticked by, she felt worse and worse. Why wasn't the train leaving? Had someone from the cult figured things out? Even worse, had they pinned last night's attack on her?

Were the police on their way right now to pick her up and throw her in jail? Bile splashed the back of her throat and she fought against the urge to vomit. She had to stay in her seat. *Had to.*

Finally, after she was so racked with nerves she wanted to scream, the wheels squealed against the rails, and the train chugged northward. Despite her grim imaginings, her car was still mostly empty. As she sank deeper into her seat and drew her hood low over her eyes, Megan dared to let herself hope. She'd made it this far. Maybe, just maybe, she'd escape to start a new life.

One where she'd make better choices.

THE PHONE JANGLED AGAIN. Loud and strident, it made Les' sensitive lupine hearing ache. It took him a moment to realize he needed his human form to make the noise go away. He'd tried to ignore the damned thing, but whoever was calling wouldn't give up. Every time he ventured near the house, it was ringing. With an aggravated growl, he commanded his body to shift.

As soon as he had feet rather than paws, he strode through the door of his cabin deep in the woods, jaw tight with annoyance. The remote location a few miles outside Rocky Mountain House often lost phone service for long periods of time.

"Yes and too bad this isn't one of them," he muttered, snatched up the receiver, and barked, "Yes, I'm here."

"It's about damned time. I've been trying to get hold of you for days."

Les' eyes widened. "Jed?"

"Who the hell else?"

Les brayed laughter. "Good point. It's not as if very many people have this number. What's up, boss? I thought you were coming my way months ago. The boys and I wondered what happened."

"Now that I have your attention, hang up." Jed's voice held a sharp edge that Les remembered all too well. "We'll do this a more private way."

"You got it." Les dropped the black receiver back into place. He kicked the door shut to keep the cold breeze out. It didn't bother him as a wolf, but he was naked, and the air had a chill edge to it. He trotted into the bedroom and had begun to dress when Jed's voice sounded in his mind.

"Where the hell have you been? I've been trying to reach you for a week."

Les sank onto the bed and pulled a quilt over his still-bare legs as he considered where to start. Jed was clan leader for wolf shifters. He needed all the information Les could provide. *"First off, we're all still okay."*

"That's a relief. When I couldn't raise you, I was afraid Hunters had killed everyone. Made me half-crazy not to know anything. Anyway, we pulled into Calgary last night, so I'm finally close enough to use telepathy."

"Is your new mate with you?"

"Affirmative. Bron, Terin, and Alice are with me." Jed blew out a breath. *"You may have heard through the grapevine, we'd originally decided to come north as part of our wedding trip, but Hunters nabbed half a dozen of us in northern California. It took a major offensive to free our people. Even so, we lost a couple."*

Les nodded, and then realized Jed couldn't see him. "Yes, I

know. We've had problems of our own. Hunters almost got your cousins, Ron and Chris. We killed them, and I'm still waiting for the fallout on that one since we also killed the whole posse that came afterward, hunting for their fallen companions. All five of them."

"How many total? Was there any choice?" Jed's voice was stern as he peppered Les with questions.

"Seven. No, no choice." Anger tightened Les' muscles. He'd like to kill every goddamned Hunter in the universe, but he wasn't about to tell Jed that. And there hadn't been any choice, not really. They'd been surrounded. The only thing that saved them was taking a firm offensive position.

Jed broke into Les' thoughts. *"What'd you do with the bodies?"*

"Don't worry, boss. No one will ever find them. We dragged them to the very bottom of a cave system where there's a vent to an upper cave and burned them."

"How long ago?"

Les thought about it. He'd spent much of the last month as a wolf, which skewed his time sense. *"Maybe a week."*

"You still haven't told me why you weren't answering your phone."

"We've all been in our wolf forms. There's a fire burning out of control between our pack and the crest of the Rockies. A couple of the cabins farther west incinerated—"

"Humph," Jed interrupted, obviously not concerned about an out-of-control wildfire. *"Any of you find mates yet?"*

"What do you think? It's not as if the odds are in our favor."

"Maybe Alice can change that. Women trust her. She's actually scared up three mates since she joined Bron, Terin, and me." A hesitation. *"How close did you say that fire was?"*

"My cabin's not in any immediate danger. It's fall and I'm expecting it to rain soon." Les scratched at month-old beard growth on his chin. *"It's pretty primitive here, boss. Nothing like your digs in Hollywood."*

A different voice sounded in his head—rich, vibrant, and definitely female. *"I've been listening in. Shameless of me not to have said something earlier. Don't worry about me. My life was a whole lot simpler before I met up with Jed and my other two mates. Besides, I'm looking forward to meeting the clan members here in Alberta."*

Les' mouth twitched into half a smile. *"You must be Alice. We've heard a lot about you. Are you really six feet tall?"*

Alice snorted, making Les wish he'd kept his mouth shut. After all, Alice was mated to his clan leader. *"How about if we leave the details open, and you can see for yourself when we get there? Jed says it's a four or five hour drive, and we should arrive sometime tomorrow. Is there anything we need to bring from the big city?"*

Les gazed around his one bedroom cabin as if he expected a grocery list to materialize. He cleared his throat before remembering he didn't need his actual voice. *"Um, we've been pretty much living off the land this past month, so anything you bring would be welcome."*

"I get the picture." Jed broke in with a laugh. *"We'll fill up the trunk and the rest of the back seat."*

Les couldn't help himself. *"Who gets to sit next to Alice?"*

Female chuckling made his heart lighter than it had been in a long time. *"Oh, they fuss and snarl a bit, but they sort of take turns. It's nice actually, to have three doting mates."*

"I'm sure it is." Les brushed a wave of sadness aside. He'd love to have a woman to fuss over, alongside Karl, his pack mate. They'd hunted for years for a female to grace their lives without success after their first mate died in childbirth in the 1600s. A few promising candidates crossed their path when they'd lived in Edmonton, but Hunters had driven them out of the city fifty years before.

"We'll be there by tomorrow afternoon." Jed's voice was gruff,

and Les figured his clan leader could read his mind.

"I'll alert the troops, boss. Everyone will be really glad to see all of you. And to meet your mate."

Les waited, but a certain emptiness told him Jed had signed off. He shoved the quilt aside, finished dressing, and called Karl through their telepathic link. It didn't take long before paws scrabbled against the door, and Les remembered he'd shut it. By the time he crossed the small space and pulled the door open, Karl had found his human form and stood shivering, arms wrapped around his tall, spare frame. Black hair hung to his waist in tangles.

"Thanks. Damned cold out here." The wolf shifter bounded into the room, giving the door a shove as he passed through it. "What's up?"

"Jed's here." Les spread his arms wide and rolled his eyes. "Along with his lieutenants and their new mate. We've got to clean this place up."

"Why? It's always been good enough for us."

Les slugged him in the arm. "You weren't listening. Jed's mate will be here."

"Oh, I get it." Karl chortled, his dark eyes gleaming with glee. "Maybe if we didn't do anything, she'd take pity on us and—"

"Right. Find some clothes, and we'll get to work. I don't think Jed, Terin, or Bron will want their new mate waiting on the likes of us."

Karl sprinted for his sleeping alcove toward the rear of the log cabin's main room. Drawers banged open. "Fire's getting closer," he called over one shoulder. "Maybe it would be better for all of us to get together in Red Deer."

Les considered it. "Nope. Too soon since we axed those Hunters. That's where they were from—there and Edmonton. I don't want any friendly sheriff asking questions if they discover we live out here. Are you sure the fire's closer? Maybe the wind just shifted direction."

"It's definitely closer. The smoke's thicker, and I can actually hear it burning from the rise a couple miles west of here. At least my wolf can." Karl slid his legs into trousers and pulled a sweater over his head before shoving his feet into an ancient pair of sheepskin slippers. He turned to Les. "Where do you think we should start? Come to think of it, when do you want to alert the rest of the clan, or should I do that?"

"We can take care of that later tonight. How about if you work on the dishes? I'll sweep and get the kettle going for laundry."

Karl strode to the sink and pumped the handle for water. "Eww." He wrinkled his nose. "How long have these plates been here?"

"Does it matter?" Les lugged a large, cast iron kettle in through the back door and hefted it onto a wood-burning stove. He opened the firebox door, levered a pocket knife out of his pants, and started shaving tinder. "Let's warm some water. That should help." As he worked, Les dialed in his lupine senses and scented fresh air coming through the back door. It was indeed tinged with smoke. What bad timing for a major fire. If it drove them into one of the nearby towns, they'd risk discovery because Hunters could scent them.

"Les?"

He looked up from his half-built fire. "Um-hum."

"Maybe it's time to move on."

"No!" Les banged a fist down on his thigh. "I'm sick of running. If the fire gets this far, we'll come back when it's over and rebuild."

"But we'll never find a mate out here."

"Just do the damned dishes. We've got enough problems without adding to them."

www.ingramcontent.com/pod-product-compliance
Lightning Source LLC
Chambersburg PA
CBHW060746210726
48292CB00015B/2794